SENTIMENTAL JOURNEY

SENTIMENTAL JOURNEY

THE CABIN OF LOVE & MAGIC: BOOK 3

JOANNE PENCE

QUAIL HILL PUBLISHING

Quail Hill Publishing

PO Box 64

Eagle, ID 83616

Visit our website at www.quailhillpublishing.net

First Quail Hill Publishing E-book: January 2021

First Quail Hill Publishing Print Book: January 2021

ISBN: 978-1-949566-41-3

SENTIMENTAL JOURNEY

CHAPTER 1

Julia Perrin lifted the cat carrier from her Jeep. "We're here, Otis, and I'll spring you from jail soon as I'm sure it's safe. Don't worry, little guy, things will look up soon. Or so I hope."

She unlocked the door to the family cabin in Garden Valley, Idaho. She owned it jointly with her two half-sisters, Carly Fullerton-Townson and Mallory Conway. Or, at least, she'd been told they were her half-sisters. Julia couldn't help but wonder if the hospital hadn't switched her at birth because while her mother and sisters were tall, buxom, and beautiful, she was short, with a slight build, and—she believed—quite plain. Her ash blond hair was twisted into a single braid that reached halfway to her waist, while large cobalt blue eyes were framed by surprisingly dark brows and lashes given how pale her hair was. She rarely wore make-up and preferred baggy, comfortable clothes. At age thirty-five, she was the oldest of the three sisters. She had never married, never came close to marrying and, frankly, had never met anyone she wanted to marry.

Julia entered the cabin's foyer, glanced at the stairs that led up to three bedrooms and a full bathroom, and continued past them to the great room.

She unzipped the cat carrier. "Come out, Otis. You'd better get used to being here."

Otis was a gray and white tuxedo cat—a very friendly, affectionate little guy. But for some reason, instead of springing from his cat carrier the way he usually did, he poked his head out and then shrank back inside and hissed.

"What's with you, cat?" Julia said. She lifted him from the case and petted him, telling him all would be fine. She filled a bowl with water for him and put Otis and the bowl on the floor in the kitchen area. But the cat scooted behind a chair, his eyes wide and round.

Julia shook her head. Most likely, the long car ride from her apartment in Bend, Oregon, had upset him. He usually was curious, not scared.

She looked around the room and had to admit the cabin looked no worse for wear, despite her sister Mallory having run it as a bed and breakfast for the past few months.

Some months earlier, Mallory, who answered letters addressed to "Dear Nellie" in her advice to the lovelorn column called "Misery Loves Company," wrote of a cabin that might house some ghosts who enjoyed the decidedly unghostly habit of helping visitors find true love.

Mallory even gave the cabin a name, calling it "The Cabin of Love and Magic."

When a newspaper article "exposed" the location of Mallory's "Cabin of Love and Magic," an avalanche of interest followed. People wanted to book a room. Lots of people. Single people.

Julia imagined many of them believed life would be much easier if some disembodied spirit could find love for them. It was certainly easier than the usual way, a way paved with heartache and wasted time when one's supposed love god or goddess turned from angelic into a sleazy, unfaithful demon.

Or sometimes, as in Julia's case, when true love never emerged at all.

Not that she was looking.

Julia remembered how she had hated the idea when Mallory announced she wanted to turn the cabin into a bed and breakfast. But so far, the gambit was actually making money. Not a lot, but it was better than nothing. And no one had, as yet, threatened to sue when they didn't find the love they sought.

Of course, with only two guest rooms, it wasn't as if Mallory had had to deal with a lot of people. And she knew how to make each guest feel important and welcome. But Mallory suddenly had other things on her agenda—most of all, a handsome veteran named Gunnar McDermott as well as the growing popularity and demands on her advice column—and she could no longer fit running a bed and breakfast into her increasingly busy life.

That created a dilemma for the three sisters. Mallory wondered if they shouldn't close the B&B and either sell the cabin or find someone else to manage it as a simple vacation rental.

But since Julia had recently lost her job due to downsizing, she volunteered to run the bed and breakfast herself.

Even over the telephone, Julia could sense her sisters' reluctance to agree to her idea. They'd both, at times, bore the brunt of her acerbic personality. It wasn't, she liked to say, that she was cranky or bossy or unwilling to compromise, but she was overly honest—and some people couldn't handle that. Still, she understood why her sisters felt she and "the hospitality industry" weren't a match made in heaven.

Julia pointed out to them that without a job her savings were dwindling. She had to do something, so why not take over running the B&B? At least it offered a roof over her head—a free roof, in fact, since she was *a part owner* of the cabin. Knowing what she was like when she dug in her heels, her sisters didn't even try to argue.

So Julia gave up her apartment, and here she was.

She turned to the portrait of Elijah Donnelly over the fireplace. He was the cabin's builder and one of the three "matchmaking" ghosts said to lurk there.

He looked like a young 1890s farmer dressed in his Sunday best. His blond hair was parted slightly off-center and slicked down straight. He wore a gray jacket with a white carnation in the lapel, a vest, tie, and a white shirt whose collar must have been starched to a torturous degree the way it stood upright on his neck. His eyes were an unusual shade of blue. Others often called them lavender, which made Julia question their color aptitude.

"Well, Elijah," she said aloud, hands on hips, "you're finding this all quite amusing, aren't you? Or you would be if there were such things as ghosts, which we all know there are not. But a fool and his money are soon parted, and let's hope plenty of fools coming out here to stay at"—she shuddered—"the Cabin of Love and Magic."

She really hated that name.

She proceeded to unload her Jeep. She'd sold her furniture and had given away everything she couldn't sell, so she hadn't had much to pack. The only important items were her laptop and printer. She had been a graphic designer for a small tech company, and after losing her job, she had thought it would be easy to find one similar. But at the moment, the need for graphic designers had diminished due to changes in the economy. For now, she could only get small work-at-home gigs that brought in equally small pay. But they were better than no pay at all.

She carried her boxes upstairs. She knew Mallory had used the smallest bedroom and rented the other two. She would do the same.

As she unpacked, she heard a soft whistling sound. She stepped into the hallway to find the shrill noise even louder.

Hurrying down the stairs, the "toots" became a high, loud screech, and once in the great room, it sounded just like...

She stopped and gaped. A tea kettle sat on the stove, steam shooting from its spout and its whistle growing higher and more ear-splitting with each passing second.

She ran to it and shut off the burner.

On the kitchen island sat a teacup and saucer. A tea bag of Earl Grey, her favorite, lay beside it, plus a spoon and a sugar bowl.

"What in the world?" Her eyes searched the room. Otis once again cowered in the cat carrier.

With a hard swallow, she swiveled around to gawk at the tea service. She hadn't set all that up ... had she? Was someone else in the cabin?

She checked the French doors that led from the great room to the back porch. Locked. She went to the small hall off the foyer that led to the laundry room, a half-bath, and the door to the garage. That door was also locked.

But she had left the front door unlocked. She shuddered at the thought that someone might have entered while she was upstairs. Could he, or she, be inside now?

She stepped out onto the front stoop. The cabin had been built on a dirt road that edged the Middle Fork of the Payette River. The area had been isolated when the cabin was first built and remained so. Her Jeep sat on the driveway, but no other car was in view, and no other homes were near the cabin.

Julia couldn't imagine anyone sneaking inside to make her a cup of tea. Could one of her sisters be playing games to scare her about the so-called, albeit nonexistent, ghosts?

"Carly? Mallory? This isn't funny!" she called, marching around, and even going onto the back porch and looking over the fenced land behind the house.

All was silent ... and seemed quieter than ever. Julia's breathing quickened, but she steeled herself. She'd never been a namby-pamby, scaredy-cat type, and she wasn't about to start now.

The only explanation was that she had set up the tea service herself and somehow forgot she'd done it.

Otis had come out of his carrier, inched a little closer to her, and now sat in the middle of the room, giving her a quizzical look. She picked him up and hugged him.

Unbidden, her gaze lifted again to the portrait of Elijah Donnelly. He seemed to be staring straight at her and his expression, instead of his usual stoic smile, seemed to be a smirk.

Julia's knees felt wobbly. She put down Otis and turned away, not wanting to look anymore at Elijah, and dropped onto a barstool by the kitchen island. Her imagination was clearly working overtime.

The long drive from Oregon hadn't only made her cat nervous and skittish. It had done the same to her.

Jean-Philippe Fontaine realized he was every bit as crazy as his few remaining relatives claimed as he drove north along a two-lane highway with a fast-moving, boulder-filled river on one side of him and ear-popping high mountains on the other.

He was a slim man, not quite six feet in height, with a

narrow face, prominent nose, a stubble of a beard, and wavy brown hair. He was as French as his name, but since he had spent many years while growing up traveling back and forth between Paris and New York City, he was proficient in English and knew quite a bit about the United States. Not Idaho, however. This was the first time he'd traveled there.

He didn't know what he would have done without a GPS because the roads he was supposed to turn on were narrow and not well marked. He had expected much larger roads, especially when he reached a town with the bizarre name of Crouch. He didn't know if it was called that because it had been some pioneer's last name, because back when there was gold in the Payette River miners had to crouch down to pan for it, or if it was simply a play on grouch, which was how he was feeling when his GPS decided it could not find his destination.

He would have stopped at a gas station and asked for help, except that he didn't see any gas station in the town.

He was also hungry.

The wooden building housing a brew pub called The Rusty Nail looked as if it had been there forever. It seemed the sort of place he could not only get something to eat, but something strong to wash it down. Hopefully, between food and ale, his mood would improve.

He found parking in front of the restaurant. He might have considered that not a good sign as far as the tastiness of its food, but he noticed that just about every establishment in the small town had parking nearby. From the street, he stepped up onto a wooden sidewalk under an overhanging roof. It was as if he'd been transported into the Old West.

An ice-cold breeze reminded him that winter was fast approaching. He hurried into The Rusty Nail and was struck by the scent of charred hamburgers, fries, beer, and whiskey. Pockets of men in cowboy hats, as well as a few women, sat at tables, booths, or the large, Western-style bar. He wouldn't have been surprised to see Wild Bill Hickok playing a not-so-friendly game of five-card stud with Buffalo Bill Cody. Quickly removing his tie, he stuck it in his sports coat pocket, unbuttoned his shirt's top button, and took a seat at the bar.

As the bartender walked up to him, a grin formed under his bushy mustache. "Glad to see you're making yourself comfortable. This isn't exactly a necktie kind of place."

"No, I can see. I like your establishment. It has character."

The white-haired fellow looked pleased by the compliment. "And I hear an accent. Where you from, stranger?"

"France. And I'm happy to visit this part of the world."

"Well, then, welcome. What can I get you?"

Different drinks went through Jean-Philippe's mind, but he didn't want to seem too out of place. "I'll have whatever is on tap."

The bartender's eyebrows rose the slightest bit, but he poured a pint of pale ale and set it on the counter.

"*Merci.*" Jean-Philippe took a sip and found it refreshing.

"Are you here for the hunting or fishing?" the bartender asked.

"Neither one. I'm here to see nature."

"Well, the name's Butch."

Jean-Philippe nodded. "I'm Jean-Philippe."

Butch's eyes squinted a bit at the name. "Pleased to meet you. You plan to stick around a while or just passing through?"

"If the area is as I hope, I will stay awhile."

"It's a nice little town. Quiet this time of year, not like summer when the place is jumping, relatively speaking. Hope you like it. If you have questions about anything, just stop by and I'll see if I can help."

"That's very kind," Jean-Philippe said. "For now, all I need is a menu." He soon ordered a cheeseburger and what Americans bizarrely called "French" fries. A little later, he caught Butch's eye again, reached into his inside jacket pocket, and took out a folded news story. "I do have a question. I'm looking for this house, or 'cabin' as it is called. Do you know this place?"

Butch looked at the news article titled "Dear Nellie's Cabin of Love and Magic Exposed!" and chuckled. "Oh, yes. I've seen this before." His eyebrows rose as he eyed the Frenchman. "But you're a handsome young fellow. You don't strike me as the type of guy who needs ghosts to help him find women."

Jean-Philippe grinned. "No, I'm curious about the cabin. Nothing more. And definitely I'm not here looking for love."

Butch smirked. "Well, that's good because this article isn't completely on the up and up. I mean, the cabin is just a little house along the river. There's nothing magical about it. And I really doubt it has any ghosts."

"I don't think I'd like to go to a place that has real ghosts. Or magic. No, I have my own reasons for wanting to see the house."

"Well then, you need to head north on the Middlefork Road." Butch explained some of the houses and signs he would pass before reaching a dirt road on the right heading toward the river. It would lead him right to the cabin. "It looks like the photo, only older. Old log house, two stories."

"Do you know the Donnelly family?" Jean-Philippe asked, refolding the newspaper article and tucking it back in his pocket.

"I've met two of the girls, the younger ones. The oldest one has come in here a time or two, but she's not your friendly, talkative type. She orders, sits in a corner by herself, eats, then leaves."

"And do they all live in the cabin?"

"Never did live there together that I've heard. One got married, moved down to Boise. Another was living there and then took up with a local fellow. Now, word has it that the oldest sister is there all by herself. She's, I hear, an odd one."

"Odd?"

"So they say."

Jean-Philippe's eyebrows rose, but he had more important issues than some woman's peculiar character. "But tell me, did you know any of the earlier Donnellys?"

"Years ago, I knew the girls' mother, Roxanne Donnelly. She was something else. Real pretty. One of those personalities that when she walked into a place, you couldn't take your eyes off her. She was a singer, a really good singer. She used to perform in musicals all over the country. Meant she wasn't around much to take care of her girls, but at least she'd bring them here for a month each summer. She'd often sing at special events in town, barbecues, Independence Day celebrations and all, and she'd substitute if needed when our local group performed a musical. Of course, when she'd perform, it'd always be a sell-out. But then, one year, she didn't show up—and never came back after that. Nobody really knew why, or if they did know, they didn't say."

"Is she no longer alive?"

"Right. When she died, her daughters inherited the cabin and fixed it up. Ah! Here's your food. I'll stop jawing so you can enjoy your meal."

A waitress set the burger in front of him, and Butch refilled his beer.

As Jean-Philippe ate, he thought about all the bartender had told him.

CHAPTER 2

Abracing chill in the air was a definite harbinger of winter. Julia put on her hiking boots and an Army-Navy surplus store quilted jacket and left the cabin. She was a devoted camper, although she usually slept in the back of her Jeep rather than in a tent. Whenever she came to the cabin, one of the first things she did was to walk down to the nearby river. The path took her through air scented with ponderosa pines, firs, cottonwood trees, and thick shrubs while listening to the calls of a multitude of birds, particularly hawks, mallards, and Canadian geese.

Being out in nature helped her relax, and since arriving at the cabin, she needed that. Suddenly appearing cups of tea and smirking portraits had left her nerves jangled, although not as badly as when she thought about having to deal with bed and breakfast customers. Now, faced with the reality of running a bed and breakfast, she wondered what in the world she'd been thinking. She scarcely knew how to cook. How was she supposed to serve strangers breakfast? And what, in heaven's name, was she supposed to say to them?

Her sisters had been right when they'd questioned her ability to do this.

Before long, she caught a glimpse of the glittering river as it wound its way along marshy banks. Beyond the river, jagged mountains stood, their foliage gone with the approaching winter. Hints of snow already powdered the crests of the highest peaks, foretelling the coming of winter and the Christmas season. But for now, the late fall landscape had a stark beauty that she loved.

As her gaze returned to the path she walked, she was startled to see a man standing a short distance before her.

He took off his tan, wide-brimmed cowboy hat, and smiled at her. "Julia! Hello! I was wondering if you would ever return."

"My goodness! Luke!" She smiled back. "How nice to see you again." She had met him in June when she briefly visited her sister, Carly, who had been staying at the cabin. After that meeting, Julia had only seen Luke once more when she was leaving the cabin to return home, and he gave her a posy of wildflowers. She found him an interesting and likable fellow, and thoughts of him had come unbidden to her from time to time over these past months, but at the same time she found something a bit strange about him. Of course, that could have been simply from living out in this emptiness and taking care of elderly parents.

He put his hat back on and waited in silence for her to join him.

As she stepped closer, she remembered how unconventional his appearance was.

His eyes were gray and deep set, while he wore his brown hair unfashionably long. His cheekbones were broad, his nose high and straight, but his skin, although tanned, had a gaunt, fragile look to it and his body was unnaturally thin, as if he had suffered a long, debilitating illness.

His clothes were every bit as anti-fashion as hers were. They looked like Farmer's Almanac rejects from many years ago: brown slacks, a heavy bleached-muslin shirt, and old-man suspenders. But they looked right on him, almost endearing. Very *Little House on the Prairie,* if she were being honest.

"How have you been?" he asked when she caught up and they walked together.

"Well enough. You?"

"Same as always," he said.

"And your parents?" she asked. "You said you look after them. Are they doing all right?"

He faced her with those gray eyes that seemed able to see right into her soul. It was disconcerting, even a bit unnerving, and she turned back to focus on the path on which they walked. "It's kind of you to have remembered them," he said. "They're well. Sometimes I think they're healthier than I am."

A felled log lay on the beach. She heard Luke lightly wheeze and remembered when they first met he mentioned some breathing issues as a result of his time in the military. "Why don't we sit?" she asked.

"Let's." He sat on the log and she took a spot beside him. They both faced the water, which now took on a greenish-gray hue in the late afternoon light.

"You mentioned that you're a neighbor," she said. "So why don't I see any homes near my cabin?"

He watched the flow of the river. "Perhaps I don't live as close as I suggested. But I like this area, so I come here often. It's an easy enough walk."

"A mile or so?" she asked.

"Something like that."

She eyed him. Something was off for sure, but he was a private person. Since she was as well, she could respect that. And for some reason she found his company pleasant, despite her normally being wary of any "mysterious strangers" such as he. The weirdest thing was that she felt sympathetic, even protective, of him ... which were not emotions she normally felt toward anyone. Ever.

"Your farm must keep you busy," she suggested, studying him.

"A bit. What about you? Are you here on vacation, or is this another quick trip?"

She put her hands on her knees. "I stupidly volunteered to run the cabin as a bed and breakfast. Turns out it's my turn since my sisters are both too busy, thanks to the cabin having found them true love."

"The cabin did what?" His eyes filled with curiosity.

She scrunched her mouth. "I was joking. What I should have said is that my sisters came to the cabin and while there, they found love."

"Oh?" He cocked an eyebrow. "And now you're staying there..."

"But *not* to find love." She tucked a loose strand of hair behind her ear. "Trust me, love is not anything I'm looking for."

A small frown line appeared between his eyebrows, but then he turned back to the river. "I see."

This turn in the conversation was making her uncomfortable. She returned to a safe subject—her sisters. "You might remember me saying when I was here last time, it was to make sure my sister, Carly, was okay. Well, not only was she okay, she fell in love with her lodger."

"That's good, isn't it?" he asked, looking a bit worried.

Julia chuckled. "It's very good. Carly and Alex got married after only a month, and now live in Boise where she just opened a landscaping business and nursery, and Alex is working on his next book. Then, after that, my baby sister, Mallory, came to the cabin, met an old childhood friend, and they fell in love."

The outer edges of Luke's eyes crinkled with delight. "And now they're married, too?"

"Well, no, although they should be. But Mallory has had several bad experiences while engaged and doesn't like to think of marriage. Then, out of the blue, she phoned me and said that she and her fellow, his name's Gunnar, have found a house to rent." Julia stopped talking. She had no idea why she was telling all this to a stranger. It wasn't like her at all.

"And that's why you're here?" he asked.

"Basically. The two are now spending a week in Montana for no good reason that I can figure. I seriously have no idea what's going on with them."

"But at least you're back," he said

"Right. I'll get to take care of lodgers and serve them breakfasts. Not exactly my idea of fun."

He tried to look serious, but it wasn't working. "I would imagine."

"Are you mocking me?" Her voice was stern, but she couldn't stop a smile.

He raised his hands. "Never."

"You'd better not be," she said, working hard to stop grinning. She glanced at her watch. "I should head back to the house. I've got to go to the grocery and get stocked up on things I like to eat. Mainly microwavable and pre-cooked."

He seemed to ponder that a moment, then nodded. He joined her on the walk back to the cabin. When they reached her driveway he asked, "Do you think you'll be coming down to the river again tomorrow?"

The ground seemed to tilt at his words. She couldn't remember the last time a man indicated he might want to see her again. Usually she scared them off so fast, they all but ran to get away from her. Where had she gone so wrong with this fellow? Well, she did think he was strange...

She didn't know what to say, but the words fell from her lips. "I'll try to, probably late morning."

"I'll be there." He touched the brim of his hat and walked away.

She hurried into the cabin.

Not until she was inside did she think about him continuing down the dirt road in front of the cabin, but in the opposite direction from the main roadway in the area. She hadn't gone that way since she was young. Back then, the road dead-ended because nothing was out there.

She guessed it had changed.

———

Jean-Philippe drove his Audi rental into the driveway of the only house in the area and parked beside an ancient Jeep. Glancing from the news article to the surprisingly small, rustic, two-story log house before him, he saw he was at the right location, but it didn't look like anything that would be called a "cabin of love and magic."

He knocked. A woman opened the door. She looked about his age—mid-thirties, and she was petite, reaching no higher than his chin. Her hair was so light it was almost white, and she wore it with a side part and pulled back off her face. Her features—a pert nose, full mouth, and flashing greenish-blue eyes—would have been attractive if she weren't scowling at him as if he were a cross between a door-to-door salesman and an ax murderer.

"Hello," he said cheerfully.

Her scowl deepened. "Who are you?"

It wasn't the greeting he expected from a bed and breakfast owner, but then, she didn't look like any B&B owner he'd ever seen in those baggy, tanned cargo pants that seemed to have something bulging from every pocked, and an oversized white sweatshirt that was not only rumpled, but spotted with what looked like mustard and ketchup.

"I heard this is a bed and breakfast," he said, still smiling.

"Yes, it is," she replied cautiously, then folded her arms.

"I suppose I should have called first, but I was anxious to get here."

She straightened her back even more than the stiff military-like posture she'd already assumed and lifted her chin. "Why?"

He blinked. How many reasons did most people have for showing up at an inn? "My apologies. I'm looking for a place to stay for a few days," he said, and then delivered the line he'd practiced for a situation just like this. "I'm a biologist, and I'm doing research on raptors with the Peregrine Foundation in Boise. I'll be spending time in the Boise National Forest and your B&B is close to it."

Her brow crossed. "Is this a joke?"

His eyebrows lifted nearly to his hairline. She was definitely the "odd" one the bartender had warned him about. "No. I assure you."

"You study raptors?"

"Falcons, hawks … I'm specializing in the gyrfalcon at the moment."

Her mouth wrinkled in annoyance. "I know what raptors are, I just didn't know people came to this area to study them. I mean, it's not like they aren't *all over the place* around here."

What was with her? Was she purposefully trying to keep him away from her inn? What was she hiding? His patience vanished. "Trust me, people study raptors. Do you have a room or not?"

She sucked in her breath. "The problem is I just arrived here myself," she said finally, and then opened her arms wide and glanced down at her rumpled clothes. "As you can see, I'm a mess. I drove for hours to get here today, and I'm not, I mean, the house is not ready for guests. Maybe tomorrow. Or better yet, the day after that."

Or never, he thought. Still, her sudden frankness jarred him. His eyes met hers and he watched hers widen in surprise, but then drop. And in that moment the idea struck that she wasn't actually angry and arrogant, but nervous—and perhaps more than a little shy—and trying to hide it with bluster. His stance softened. "I'm sorry. Please excuse my intrusion, *mademoiselle*. Or, should I say, *madam?*"

She looked rattled. "No problem. The name's Julia Perrin. Unmarried." Her cheeks reddened, and she seemed even more uneasy. Yet, he found something about her surprisingly riveting. He liked her voice, which was low with a slight, disarming huskiness to it. He ran his hand through his hair, having no idea whatsoever why he was having such a reaction to such a harsh and peculiar woman.

He gave a nod and, although he guessed he should simply leave, he couldn't. Everything was so completely different from what he had expected, he had to ask. "Tell me, the bed and breakfast that had been recommended to me is a house once owned by a family with the name Donnelly. Is this the Donnelly house?"

Her eyebrows rose. "It is."

He nodded. "Are you, by chance, a Donnelly?"

Her mouth tightened and he could almost see a wall of caution go up around her. "Why are you asking?"

"Mere curiosity."

Her face hardened and she all but spat out the words. "My mother was Roxanne Donnelly."

Her reaction to his simple question puzzled him. "I will come back when you're ready to receive guests." He then headed down the walk to his Audi.

CHAPTER 3

J ulia woke with a start. She was lying on the sofa and the room had turned cold. She sat up, and soon, the memory of where she was and why came back to her.

What a strange afternoon it had been. Not only had she run into Luke, her neighbor, a gentle and strangely fragile man whose company she enjoyed, but then a drop-dead gorgeous man had shown up on her doorstep.

She could almost believe there was something magical about this cabin!

After the raptor biologist left, she had made herself a dinner of canned stew and microwaved dinner rolls, which was pretty pathetic but fast and easy. She never claimed to be a cook. Then she'd built a fire and stretched out on the sofa with her laptop to work on one of the gigs she'd been given. Otis soon joined her.

She must have fallen asleep because the laptop was now on the floor, the lights were still on, and the fire was nearly out.

And strangest of all, instead of Otis beside her, she saw the little female calico cat that had shown up when Mallory was living at the cabin. "Pumpkin," Julia whispered, petting the cat on the head. "Where did you come from?"

She knew Otis didn't like other cats and was probably hiding under a bed upstairs.

She got up and put more logs into the fireplace, but instead of heading up to bed, she found a spare blanket, shut off the lights, and lay back down on the sofa. She knew the bedrooms would be icy cold since she hadn't bothered to turn up the heater after dinner. Besides, the firelight was pleasant.

But now that she was awake, her gaze went to Pumpkin. How had the cat gotten into the house?

She must have snuck in as Julia stood at the door and talked to the good-looking foreigner. She'd loved his accent. It sounded French. But why was he so curious about the Donnelly family? She couldn't help but suspect he knew about the cabin and the Donnelly ghosts, despite his story about the cabin being near the forest. But she couldn't imagine he needed ghosts to help him find love. So what was his reason for showing up here?

If she'd been thinking straight, she'd have made a reservation for him, or at least gotten his name and phone number. On the other hand, she'd probably managed to alienate him completely with her comments on raptors, and she'd never see him again.

She guessed she had a lot to learn about running a B&B. Somehow, she'd figure it out and get through this, just as she had every other obstacle in a long life of setbacks.

She shut her eyes.

Pumpkin seemed to sense she was feeling blue and snuggled against her, the little cat's presence warm and comforting.

She had no idea if she'd been asleep or just had her eyes shut when she heard a male voice.

"You'll be fine. You're safe here."

She opened her eyes to see, near her feet, a man perched on

the arm of the sofa. His hair was slicked down from a slightly off-center part, and his clothes ... She bolted upright.

She immediately knew why he looked so familiar. *This is a dream. I'm still sleeping. It's just a dream.*

Pumpkin walked over to the man and sat near him. He smiled as he ran his hand over the soft fur. Pumpkin was wary of strangers, so why was she putting up with this?

Julia rubbed her eyes. *Wake up, Julia!*

Fearfully, her gaze jumped to the portrait that hung above the mantle, but the room was so dark in the firelight she could see nothing but the outline of its frame. From where she sat, it looked like a portrait of nothing—as if the man, Elijah Donnelly, was no longer in it, but was here, now, sitting on the sofa with her. Her breathing quickened. She wanted to scream, to run, but she felt frozen to the spot.

I've had dreams before where I've been in danger and couldn't move, where I felt stuck in place. I'd tell myself to wake up. They were always nightmares. As this is. Wake up! I've got to wake up!

"You aren't dreaming." His voice was soft, low, and soothing. "You need to ease up on yourself, girl, and think about putting your life in order. Once that's done, all will be fine. But you're safe here with us. Never forget that. Now, go back to sleep."

At those words, Julia quaked, her rational mind insisting this was all a dream, all nonsense. She forced herself to lie back on the sofa even as, perhaps irrationally, what she really wanted to do was to grab her car keys and flee back to Oregon. But she kept telling herself this was all nothing but a strange dream.

And the next thing she knew, she opened her eyes to find the morning sun filling the great room with a golden glow. The fire had gone out during the night, and above the mantle, the portrait of Elijah stiffly smiled, the same as ever.

CHAPTER 4

The great room was chilly that morning since the fire had gone out. Julia sat up on the sofa and wrapped herself in the blanket. Her mind ticked off what she had to do next: warm up the cabin, shower, dress, and then eat breakfast. She needed to do anything, in fact, but to think about her bizarre nightmare. Clearly, it was the result of thinking way too much about ghosts. Despite having been welcomed by old Elijah and being told she was safe in the cabin, it was nonetheless a disturbing dream.

After a breakfast of PopTarts and coffee, she began to clean the cabin to get it ready for guests. There wasn't as much to do as she'd feared. Mallory had left the cabin close to spotless, so the work went quickly. She dusted and vacuumed the bedrooms, washing and changing all the linens. Much as she wished she didn't need to bother with all that, she wasn't here to relax. She was here to contribute to her sisters. And herself.

After finishing the upstairs, she moved on to the main floor and soon the cabin looked ready to receive guests.

Her thoughts turned again to the fellow from yesterday. If

others called to reserve rooms should she hold a room for him? Would that be silly? He hadn't asked for a reservation. But neither had she offered him one. And he did say he'd return.

She hated this. Why did she think she could run an inn, be nice to total strangers, and—worst of all—cook breakfast for them?

She needed to calm down. Glancing at the kitchen clock, she saw it was now late morning, which gave her an idea. She put a water bottle and paper towels into a tote, then went to her Jeep and took out her portable folding easel. It also had a storage compartment to carry paints, brushes, a palette, and other supplies. Studying art and learning to draw had been a side benefit of her majoring in graphic design. Oil paints were her preferred medium. She used to paint quite a bit, only giving it up when her job took up too much time and sapped any creative energy she might have.

Once she reached the riverbank, she set up her easel on the sand in a way that captured both the sparkle of the water as it wended its way south and the log where she and Luke had sat and talked.

Maybe she'd see him again.

Not, of course, that she cared one way or the other.

On the other hand, a little company out here wouldn't be a bad thing. She'd spent most days alone in Bend, Oregon, where she worked from home. But that was by choice, and right outside her apartment were people and businesses, so she never felt isolated. Life here was quite different from anything she'd experienced before. And that strange nightmare still left her a bit jittery.

She turned back to studying the scene before her. She wasn't an avant-garde painter, but preferred to realistically capture the beauty of nature. She began with the sky. Despite the cold, the sun shone bright with wisps of clouds.

"You never mentioned that you're an artist."

Julia's spirits bounded at the sound of Luke's voice. She smiled at him. "Because I'm not! But I like to play at it when I have time."

He moved to a spot where he could see over her shoulder at what she'd done, and to study the area she would be painting. "That looks like the best place to start," he said.

"Do you paint?" she asked.

"I used to. With oils, in fact. But I haven't for years and years. I'm sure I've forgotten everything I ever knew."

"Years and years? You don't look old to me. I'm not about to tell my age, but I suspect you might be younger than I am."

"I doubt that," he said with an odd twist to his lips.

She mixed some white with the blue on her brush and moved it to the canvas. "How about letting me see some of your paintings?"

"No." He slid his hands in his pockets. "Whatever I've done has been lost in the mists of time, I'm afraid."

She studied his rueful expression. "That's terrible."

He shrugged. "No great loss."

"What did you paint?"

"Still life, mostly. And portraits. Well, one portrait."

Portraits were difficult. She added some lighter blue streaks to the sky. "You should paint here with me."

He shook his head. "I don't have my paints anymore."

"Why not?"

He shrugged. "I don't know where they are, so I suspect they've dried up."

If he were anyone else, she would have said something cutting about losing track of his paints and letting them go bad. But there was something about Luke, a softness, that made her want to tread lightly when conversing with him. "Why not buy more?"

He dropped his gaze. "I don't know."

"Well, I agree that Crouch's selection is probably nil to none, but you can get them online."

His brow furrowed, but then he said, "Right."

It was almost as if he didn't believe her. "Really. They have good quality paints and canvases online that they'll ship you."

His eyebrows rose slightly. "A mail order buy?"

He couldn't be that removed from online shopping, could he? "They aren't too pricey and they'll get you started painting again."

"I'd rather simply watch you. Sorry, I keep distracting you."

"Believe me, the art world is glad I'm distracted." She decided right then and there to buy him supplies online.

"I'm glad you're here, Julia," he said, his voice gentle. "Even if it is for just a short while."

She felt flattered as she turned back to her picture. Had she told him she'd be here just a short while? She didn't remember, although he had probably assumed it since she and her sisters seemed to be taking turns running the place. "Thank you," she murmured. They fell into a mutual silence as she painted.

A bit later, her stomach growled. "Uh oh, hope you didn't hear that! Time for me to head back to the cabin for lunch," she said with a laugh, and then turned around to see what Luke had to say. To her surprise, he had already gone.

Julia returned to an empty bed and breakfast—not exactly the way to make money. She needed to get some customers soon, but how? And once she got them, what was she supposed to do with them? Maybe she should have just stuck with graphic design.

But she had learned one thing in her job with a website

provider. When you need to do something new, hire someone to teach you. In the end, it nearly always saved time and money.

She picked up her laptop and went to The Rusty Nail. It had good internet service, as opposed to the cabin which had close to none at all.

As she entered the brew pub, her gaze quickly dismissed the bar area and the bartender who gave her a nod of greeting and even looked like he had something to say to her. The last thing she wanted was to hear small town gossip or to become part of the gossip mill herself. She marched past him to an empty booth at the back of the restaurant.

Almost immediately, a waitress came by to take her order.

That done, her first action was to log onto the pub's Wi-Fi and order oil paints, brushes, canvases, and a portable easel stand. She even paid extra for next day delivery.

Then, while enjoying a juicy patty melt with fries, she searched for an instructor on how to deal with customers. She found several "customer service coaches" in the area and began calling them to ask if their instructions would apply to a bed and breakfast owner.

She expected to have to go to Boise for consultations, but when she reached Ryan Salzburg, she knew she'd found her coach. Not only had he worked with bed and breakfast owners, he owned a cabin in Garden Valley. They made an appointment for the next time he'd be in town.

She ended the call with a feeling of relief. Maybe, somehow, she could do this.

CHAPTER 5

A fter having been denied a room at the bed and breakfast the day before, Jean-Philippe had returned to Boise. To his surprise, after coming across the article about the Donnelly ghosts at "The Cabin of Love and Magic" and deciding to pay it a visit, he discovered that Boise, Idaho, was a good spot for working on his specialty, the preservation and importance of the raptor population—eagles, hawks, falcons, even the great condors. After arriving there he spent a day at the Peregrine Foundation headquarters and Boise State University's Intermountain Bird Observatory. When he mentioned to the director of the Peregrine Foundation that he planned to spend a bit of time in Garden Valley, things became a lot more interesting.

He had also visited the Idaho Historical Museum and the State Archives which were filled with all kinds of collections and government records. He had searched for several hours in both locations, but found no birth, death, or marriage records for Elijah or Lucas Donnelly of Garden Valley, Idaho.

He knew the task he'd given himself wouldn't be easy, and

maybe impossible. But after he went to the Donnelly cabin—stood in front of it and met the curious woman who was running it as a bed and breakfast—he had the overwhelming sense that he was finally on the right track. For that reason, the day after having been turned away from the cabin, he exchanged his luxurious Audi rental for a Dodge Ram four-wheel-drive truck and headed back to the Donnelly cabin, arriving there around noon.

He knocked, but no one answered. And the driveway was empty of cars.

He guessed *Miss* Perrin was out. He hoped she hadn't forgotten about him.

He decided to wait and walked along the road leading away from the cabin, but his thoughts remained with his hostess.

Odd, Butch at the Rusty Nail had called her. That was for sure, but her eyes had studied him with an obvious intelligence, and despite her slight figure, he could tell she had an internal strength about her. He also thought about how she kept scowling at him. Scowls were rarely the response he received from women.

Well, he was probably reading far too much into a brief encounter, and he'd soon learn she was vapid and boring. Lately, it seemed that was too often the result whenever he stuck a toe into the dating world, which he was doing far less often than in his early years when he was a bit of a ladies' man, truth be told. But he soon found that too many of those relationships had an emptiness to them that felt unsatisfactory to him. He didn't know if he was too picky or simply wasn't cut out for the kind of closeness most people were fortunate enough to find.

He couldn't imagine any of his recent girlfriends deciding to live out in a remote area the way Miss Julia Perrin was doing. He wondered what her story was. Why was she here?

What had gone on in her life that caused her to live there alone?

He soon found himself on a ridge. He looked out at rugged, craggy mountains circling the valley, their caps touched by a hint of snow. Below him, the river appeared a cold, pearly gray as it snaked by. The scene spoke to him, as did the cabin and, strangely, the woman in it. And he had no idea why.

As Julia approached the cabin, she saw a truck in the driveway. Not another surprise lodger, she prayed.

She was almost at the front door when she heard "Hello!"

The man who'd been there the day before seeking a room hurried toward her. He was on the dirt road past the cabin, the road she never took. "I was waiting for you," he called.

Something about him, maybe the accent, maybe the way his wind-tousled hair fell onto his forehead, maybe the intensity of his light gray eyes, caused her pulse to race as he approached. She was usually immune to men's attractiveness, but she wasn't to his. She put her hands on her hips. "You seem pretty sure I've got everything ready for you."

"Not at all." A smile deepened the laugh lines along the sides of his mouth.

She stiffened. Was he laughing at her?

"It's pretty country out here," he said, then added, "I'm *hoping* I can rent a room here today."

She scowled. He seemed to be trying to make amends. She'd take it. She had to learn to be an innkeeper, after all. "In that case ..." She opened the door wide and stepped inside. "Come in. I've got paperwork for you, then I'll show you the room. What's your name?"

"Jean-Philippe Fontaine."

"French?"

"Very," he said with a grin as he walked past her.

Lordy! She couldn't help but notice he was even better looking up close.

As they entered the great room, Pumpkin walked up to him, and blinked her strange yellow eyes a couple of time.

"I have two cats," Julia said. "I hope you aren't allergic."

"I'm not." He reached down to pet the cat. To Julia's surprise, Pumpkin allowed him to touch her.

"She's usually quite skittish," Julia told him.

"Really? I would have called her friendly." Jean-Philippe said as he ambled toward the fireplace. He suddenly rubbed his arms. "Oh, what's going on here?"

"What do you mean?" she asked.

"You didn't feel it?" he asked. "A crackling in the air?"

She looked at him strangely. "No."

He appeared taken aback by her abrupt response. "Must have just been me." He looked up and pointed toward the portrait over the mantle. "But tell me, who is that dour looking fellow?"

She snorted. "That's Elijah Donnelly. He built the cabin around 1890."

"Elijah Donnelly," he repeated. "What can you tell me about him?"

"Not much. After building this place, he passed away at a young age. Anyway, here's the paper you need to fill out. I can take a credit card. I won't run it until your stay is complete." She placed it on the dining table and handed him a pen.

"*Bon.*" He bent over the table as he wrote out his contact information, including his credit card number, then gave everything back to Julia.

"I'll show you your room," she said.

"Yes, but first, do you know who painted the Donnelly portrait?"

She hoped not all her lodgers would be as inquisitive as this fellow. "Since you've asked, it's a bit confused. People said it was painted by his son, Lucas. But Elijah died when his son was just a baby and no one ever heard that there were any photographs of him, so we don't know what the son used to paint the portrait, or if he simply painted what he assumed his father must have looked like. Of course..."

"Of course?"

She couldn't stop herself from mischievously adding, "I shouldn't bring it up, but I'm sure you'll hear that the cabin is haunted. Of course, it's nonsense. But there are those who swear Lucas saw his parents as ghosts, and that's how he could paint his father's portrait."

"Interesting," Jean-Philippe said.

"And untrue." She used her sternest voice.

Jean-Philippe seemed unbothered as he stepped right up to the fireplace and studied the portrait. "The technique is distinctive, and nothing like paintings done in Europe during this period."

"True. Not a surrealist. And not a cube in sight." The lodger had surprised her with his statement, as, judging from his expression, she had obviously surprised him with her response. "Are you an artist?" she asked.

"Not at all, but living in France, with so many fine museums, of course I took some classes to better understand what I was looking at." He said that as if taking art classes was the most common thing in the world.

"Makes sense." She also moved closer to Elijah's portrait. More softly and thoughtfully, she added, "I would call his style early twentieth century American primitive. It's natural and honest. Attention to detail but rather flat, with the artist making up the style as he went along rather than following other artists of his time. He might not have even known much about what was being done in Europe. Frankly, I love the style of this painting."

"I can see that," he said and seemed now to be paying more attention to her than the portrait which made her a bit uneasy. "Do you have other work by this artist?"

She stepped away from the fireplace. "I don't."

"It's a pity. He was good."

"Unfortunately, Lucas Donnelly died at a young age, just as his parents had. Lucas fought in World War One and came back to the cabin quite ill. He didn't live long after the war."

"Are you sure about that?" Jean-Philippe stared hard at her.

His odd reaction threw her back to the here and now. Just who did this guy think he was with all these questions about her relatives? "It's what my family has always believed." Her words were firm.

"I'm sorry to hear that." He sounded distressed which made no sense to her whatsoever. What was going on here?

"Let's go upstairs," she said. "I'll show you your room. And feel free to use the great room and even the kitchen at any time. It's well stocked with food for snacks, and drinks—non-alcoholic. But you're welcome to bring your own beer, wine, or anything else. How many days will you be here?"

"I don't know for sure. I'm working with the Peregrine Foundation and others on a special project in the Boise National Forest, and it's hard to say how long it will go on. A minimum of two weeks, I would think. And possibly a month or more."

Her mouth dropped. "Two weeks minimum? Oh, my. That's great. And I'm sure we can work out a reduced long-term rate for you." She realized she wasn't sounding exactly businesslike, and quickly added, "Of course, since I only have two rooms, I'll need some early warning when you're leaving so I'll know when I can accept other reservations."

He thought a moment. "What if I promise to give you three days' notice before I leave? Until then, the room is mine."

That, she definitely could live with. She swallowed hard, thinking what a boon this would be to her bottom line. "It's a deal."

She let him up to the river-view room and proudly opened the door. "We usually get two single people rooming together," she explained. "That's the reason for the twin beds instead of a queen."

"No problem." He bypassed the beds with their fluffy yellow and white comforters, the striped wallpaper and the cream-colored furniture, and headed straight to the window. The river peeked through the shrubs and trees from somewhere north of the cabin and then disappeared into the distance far to the south. "The view is beautiful. It's like a painting."

"It is."

"This is a good room," he said with a nod. "I like it."

"Good." She quickly left him so he could get settled. She no sooner reached the bottom of the stairs when the cabin's land line rang.

Two women were looking for a room for the next night. She told them she had one available, and they took it. Continuing to the great room, she was actually feeling positive about oper-ating the bed and breakfast—a tiny bit, at least.

CHAPTER 6

Julia dragged herself out of bed at seven the next morning. She had a breakfast buffet to prepare. Yesterday, after renting out the room, Julia had phoned her sister Carly, who had been a caterer. First, she gave Carly the great news about the long-term renter and then asked for suggestions about breakfast. Carly sent her to the grocery store with a long shopping list.

Maddeningly, she hadn't thought to ask her lodger what time he wanted breakfast until she was already in bed, so she was forced to get up early and hope for the best.

Scarcely awake, she and Otis pattered down the hall to the bathroom. She reached for the doorknob, then drew back her hand as if it were burned. She heard the shower running.

Sharing her bathroom just went from theory to practice, and she didn't like it. Also, it meant her lodger was facing the litter box in the bathroom—something else she'd forgotten to deal with.

Julia's morning shower would have to wait. She returned to the bedroom, dressed, and headed downstairs. Since her lodger was already up, she needed to put on coffee, water for tea, and put out the breakfast buffet—a variety of pastries, cereals, and fruits. All Julia needed to do was to cook eggs, bacon, or pork sausage for her lodger—whatever he wanted. She got herself a cup of coffee and anxiously awaited his appearance. She hadn't cooked breakfast for anyone since she was a teenager and sometimes made her father bacon and eggs.

Some twenty minutes later, Jean-Philippe entered the great room. He wore black slacks and a light blue pullover.

Julia stood as soon as she saw him. His clean hair all but sparkled and when he smiled his teeth were movie-star white. He definitely looked more scrumptious than the food she served.

"Good morning. Your place at the table is ready," she said, indicating the setting on the dining room table. "There's your choice of food to get started. Also, how would you like your eggs cooked? And do you prefer bacon or pork sausage?"

"Good morning." Jean-Philippe walked to the kitchen island where Julia had set up the spread. "Coffee only, please. Black," Jean-Philippe said and handed her a thermos. "I'm meeting a colleague this morning at the Boise National Forest."

"But we have all kinds of food," she said, taking the thermos. "And this is a bed *and breakfast.*"

She filled the thermos as he looked over the pastries and fruit. "If you insist," he said with a smile, then grabbed a scone, said goodbye, and hurried out the door.

Well, she thought, as she picked up a chocolate-and-walnut muffin and took a big bite, that certainly was easy.

Julia had just finished cleaning up the kitchen, Jean-Philippe's room, making his bed, and giving him fresh towels, when she heard a knock on the door.

Two women stood there, suitcases at their feet.

"You must be Nan Wickham and Crystal Gilmore," she said.

"Yes, we are," said the taller and larger of the two. "I'm Crystal. She's Nan."

The women looked like they were in their forties. "Welcome to the Donnelly House," Julia said in greeting. When she'd heard Jean-Philippe call it that when they first met, she immediately decided to adopt the name.

"It was a long drive from the airport to get here," Crystal said, taking out a tissue and dabbing her brow. "I had no idea this place was so far from civilization. And I noticed there are no streetlights. How do you drive at night?"

The smile Julia wore stiffened. "Yes, that's the benefit of being here. Completely uncivilized, with peace, quiet, and no streetlights on small dirt roads."

Crystal's eyebrows rose. "I'm not used to driving along a highway that one simple mistake could cause me to plunge into a river filled with monstrous boulders! I should think you'd warn your customers about the road here."

Julia nodded. "Sounds like a great way to drum up business." But then she forced a smile as she registered them.

Where Crystal was talkative, opinionated, and blonde with lizard green eyeshadow and a figure that implied too many cakes, pies, and chocolate shakes, Nan was her opposite in almost every way. She was kale and quinoa thin, didn't smile let alone speak, and put on make-up with a light touch. Her hair was black and straight, and her bangs reached past her eyebrows.

Julia led her two lodgers up the stairs and opened the door to a room with a view of the back orchard and the mountains in the distance. It had twin beds and was decorated with warm quilts and rustic wood furniture.

Julia didn't like the scowl on Crystal's face.

"This room is tiny." The woman sniffed.

Julia gave Crystal an iron stare. "It's a cabin, not the Taj Mahal."

If those two were an example of what her guests would be like, Julia thought as she stomped downstairs, she didn't know how long she was going to be able to put up with this innkeeper job. She had never been a people person. She really should have found a way to do nothing but work with her computer. No emotion, no snide remarks, no *humans* involved. God love it!

In the kitchen, she was stunned to see the kettle on the stove, plus a cup and saucer, spoon, and sugar bowl on the island with a bag of Earl Grey next to them. As she neared them, the kettle began to whistle.

Otis jumped up on the kitchen island to see what was going on.

"This is insane!" Julia flung her arms out at her sides. "I know you didn't put the kettle on for me, Otis, so who did?" The last time she had a cup of tea set up this way she'd been able to explain it to herself. This time, she had no such luck.

"Fine, I'll drink it!" A cup of tea, in fact, was exactly what she needed. As soon as it was steeped, she planned to take it out to the back deck where she could enjoy it in peace, freezing temperatures notwithstanding.

"And also, cat, you're going to have to stay off the kitchen island when we have guests. They probably aren't cat people, so I doubt they'll be amused by you walking on the counters that I use to prepare their food. Now, *off!*"

As Otis trotted away, he gave her a decidedly sour look.

CHAPTER 7

The early appearance of Julia's two new guests and her ensuing trip to the grocery for fresh pastries for the morning's breakfast meant she missed her usual time to meet Luke at the river. It troubled her, but she had no choice.

She spent the rest of the day trying to drum up online gigs as a graphic designer. Now, as evening fell, she was wiping off the kitchen counter after a dinner of ramen and roasted chicken from the grocery's deli, when she heard the front door open.

She froze. Although she'd given all three guests their own keys to the front door since she had no interest in playing doorman or having her guests feel they were under a curfew, it felt odd to have people simply walk in on her.

She relaxed at the sound of Crystal's blaring baritone. Both cats scattered.

"Welcome back," she said as Crystal and Nan enter the great room.

"We went to The Rusty Nail for dinner." Crystal dropped into an easy chair near the fireplace. "I doubt we'll go back there."

"It's usually pretty good. Maybe the cook was having an off day," Julia said, turning her back on them as she finished the clean-up. Did nothing please that woman? "There's coffee, tea, and sodas in the refrigerator. Help yourselves if you'd like anything."

She was surprised neither woman had replied, not even with a simple, "Thanks."

When she faced them again, she discovered why. They were too busy staring at Jean-Philippe who had just returned to the cabin as well.

Julia wasn't sure what to do. She had understood, as an owner, she was supposed to stay up in her room and let her guests feel as if they owned the place. But here she was in the great room with them.

"Isn't this nice?" Her voice sounded unnaturally high and bright to her ear. "All my guests are here at once." *Duh!* That sounded dumb. "Let me do the introductions. Jean-Philippe Fontaine, Crystal Gilmore, and Nan Wickham."

"So pleased to meet you," Jean-Philippe said and held out his hand.

Between his French accent and killer smile, Crystal and Nan looked ready to swoon, but somehow managed to shake his hand.

He then walked over to Julia who had remained by the kitchen island. His gray eyes captured hers as he handed her a bottle of Calvados. "I thought a nice after-dinner brandy with you would be a pleasant way to end my first day at the Donnelly House." He slightly cocked his head. "I trust you've already had your dinner."

She did all she could to hold his gaze although, to be honest, his gray eyes were even more disarming than when she had first met him. "Yes. Thank you."

"You can serve it over ice, if you wish. That's the way I most enjoy it," he said.

"Let's do it, then," she said.

He faced the two women who were still gaping at him. "Would you ladies care to join us?"

"Of course. So nice of you to ask," Crystal gushed, even as her eyes darted between Julia and Jean-Philippe to figure out if anything was going on between them.

"Thank you," Nan murmured meekly, her eyes wide and round.

Julia got out the glasses and ice, and Jean-Philippe poured. Julia lit a fire in the fireplace and soon all were seated in front of it. Nan and Crystal on the sofa, Jean-Philippe and Julia on the chairs, and Otis on Julia's lap, while Pumpkin sat in a corner where she could watch all of them.

Jean-Philippe faced Nan and Crystal. "So what brings you ladies to such a quiet area?"

The two glanced at each other, and then Julia. Finally, Crystal leaned toward Jean-Philippe, smiled until her dimples appeared, and replied in a stage-whisper, "The ghosts."

Jean-Philippe bent his head a little closer to her. "Ah! I've heard a bit about Donnelly ghosts." His eyes lifted to Julia.

"There are no ghosts here," she stated. "Just because this is an old cabin—"

"She doesn't want to admit it," Crystal explained to Jean-Philippe. "She might be afraid you'll dash off. But no need. These are nice ghosts. Not dangerous at all."

Jean-Philippe glanced at Julia, one eyebrow raised. "Why don't you tell all of us about the ghosts that live here?"

"They say they help visitors to the cabin find true love." Crystal smiled coyly at him.

"I've heard the rumors started with your family," Nan said, looking hopeful that Julia would talk about them.

"That's exactly what I'd like to hear," Jean-Philippe said. He smiled at Nan who looked as if she'd suddenly lost the ability to breathe.

"It's all silly," Julia said.

"Not according to the news," Crystal announced. She turned to Jean-Philippe. "That's how Nan and I learned about the cabin. We read the story of the ghosts who help people find true love in our local paper—in Chicago. So here we are. Ready, willing and able." She batted her lashes.

"I think I may have come across that article." Jean-Philippe faced Julia, his eyebrows lifted.

Now he admits it, Julia thought, again wondering just what was up with him. "Since you're all so interested, I'll tell you the story one time, and that's it." She put down her empty glass and rattled off facts like a drill sergeant facing new cadets. "The cabin was built by Elijah Donnelly for his bride when she was expecting their first child. Unfortunately, she died in childbirth. Their child, Lucas, survived. It is said that Elijah was so distraught over the death of his wife that he died within a year of her. Their son was raised by an aunt. At a young age, he joined the Army, and ended up fighting in World War I. He returned sick, and died alone in the cabin. The three of them are said to be the ghosts who haunt us. Period. End of story."

"That doesn't sound very romantic," Crystal said, her mouth scrunched as if she'd just bit into a lemon.

"Then these ghosts are not your relatives?" Jean-Philippe asked, looking puzzled. "It sounds as if they had no children."

Once again, Julia found herself both surprised and annoyed at Jean-Philippe's interest in her family. "Lucas willed the cabin to his cousin, Theodore, who was my great-grandfather."

"I see," Jean-Philippe said. "And who decided those three people have become ghosts?"

"It was Theodore," Julia explained. "He swore some sort of

ghostly intervention caused him to meet his wife, and the story spread."

"That's all?" Jean-Philippe asked.

Julia's lips pursed. "There are similar stories with other relatives." She decided to put an end to this nonsense and raised her chin. "I should warn all of you, however. There's another side to the tale."

"Another side?" Crystal asked.

Julia nodded, her expression stern. "If the ghosts find true love for you, but you reject the person they send, then you'll never be happy in love from that time on."

Crystal drew back her head. "That's a bit harsh! What if you don't like the person they send you?"

Nan's eyes widened. "It kind of reminds me of that reality show where people get married to someone they've never even seen before. And very few of those marriages continue past the first month or two."

Julia gawked at her—that was the most she'd ever heard Nan say. "I don't think ghosts work that way."

Nan seemed to slink back down into her shell, and Julia was almost sorry she'd been critical.

"I should hope not!" Crystal huffed. "I can't imagine being unhappy for the rest of my life because some ghosts have their noses out of joint when I didn't care for the fellow they found for me!"

Pumpkin suddenly let out a long, mournful wail.

The four of them jumped at the sound and then chuckled nervously.

"All right," Julia said. "Enough of all this. There are no—I repeat—no ghosts in the cabin. And so there is no way that ghosts, who don't exist, help anyone find true love. It's all fantasy. A fun story. And with that, I'm going to say goodnight." She stood.

"I, too, will go upstairs," Jean-Philippe said. "But, Julia, before you go can you tell me, what is the name of the third ghost? The woman? You didn't mention it."

She shook her head. "I've never heard."

"No? Is there no cemetery? No headstone?"

Again, Julia shook her head. "If there is, I have no idea where."

Jean-Philippe nodded as if lost in thought, then looked at Crystal and Nan and said softly, "*Bon nuit.*" He then followed Julia up the stairs.

———

It was past midnight, but Julia sat on the bed finishing a gig to design a logo. Earlier, she had tried to sleep, but her mind wouldn't shut down. Finally, she gave up, switched on her lamp, and decided to get some work done. She could use the money.

But then, out of the blue, she heard singing.

She closed the lid of the laptop, her nerves tingling.

It sounded just like her mother's voice. Her dead mother's voice. A shudder crept through her.

Her jaw clenched as she reached for her robe and put it on, then dashed to the bedroom door and opened it. Her loose, unbraided hair fell down her back and around her shoulders like a shawl.

The sound was louder, clearer now, and coming from downstairs. Julia had heard the song, "Sentimental Journey," many times as a child, and now, once more, she was hearing Roxanne sing the old ballad.

Jean-Philippe stepped into the hall, his eyes heavy with a just-awakened look. He also wore a robe. His hair was askew, the front flopping down nearly to his eyes. "Who's singing?"

"I don't know what's going on!" Julia said and practically

flew down the stairs, both annoyed and startled by her lodger's appearance, and even more so when he followed her downstairs.

All the lights, except for a night-light in the foyer, were off. Julia hurried to the great room and flipped on the light switch. Her eyes scoured the room.

The room was empty, but an old cassette player sat atop a credenza. Roxanne's voice was coming from it.

Julia ran to the machine. As Roxanne sang the words "sentimental journey," she shut off the tape—but not before her mind played the last word in the stanza, "home." She stared hard at the tape player, lost as memories washed over her at the sound of her mother's voice.

"I don't remember seeing that player there earlier," Jean-Philippe said. He stood close behind her.

She jumped at his nearness. "Me, neither." Her voice quivered. Hearing Roxanne again after so many years had unnerved her. She'd last heard her mother sing when she was eighteen, which was also the last time she, Roxanne, and her sisters were together at the cabin. She rarely referred to Roxanne as "her mother." In her opinion, the woman didn't deserve the honorific. She ran her hands through her hair, pushing it back off her face, and tried to calm herself.

Jean-Philippe gently placed his hands on her shoulders. "Are you okay?"

She drew in her breath and nodded, then stepped away, causing his hands to drop. She wasn't used to being touched, and particularly not by strangers. She rubbed her temple. "Crystal or Nan must have set it up and didn't realize they'd left it on. I don't know how it could have come back on now.... But, at least, it didn't wake them."

Jean-Philippe walked over to the Calvados bottle sitting on the coffee table. It was half gone. "I think nothing would wake them if they drank so much apple brandy after we went upstairs."

Julia rubbed her arms. "Maybe it was for the best. I can't imagine how they'd carry on if this music woke them."

Jean-Philippe smirked at that as he went to the tape player and took out the cassette. "It's a home-made tape, not commercial. It has a name. Roxanne Donnelly. Your mother, right?"

Julia took the tape. She'd never seen it before. She felt as if it were burning her fingers, and she threw it on the credenza, then stepped away from it. "My sisters told me they'd come across some old tapes Roxanne had recorded. We didn't even know they existed." Julia wondered why the construction workers who had done the renovations hadn't found the tapes earlier, but then she decided they might have forgotten to mention them to her.

"I wonder why this particular song," Jean-Philippe muttered. "That one is going to take a sentimental journey back home has many interesting connotations."

"It's irony," she said bitterly. She dropped her head, causing her hair to fall forward. She pushed it back once more and walked across the room.

"Many of us have sentimental journeys we must make." His words were soft. "And not everyone knows about their family and what happened to our ancestors the way you and your sisters seem to. Many of us don't even have a place we think of as home."

He didn't need to tell her that. She and her father had moved so many times the concept of home was all but foreign to her.

She hugged her arms tight against her stomach. She felt wide awake, and the last thing she wanted to do was to go up to her bed and lie there beset by thoughts of her mother and her childhood. She headed toward the kitchen. "I know I won't be able to sleep for a while. I'm going to stay down here, maybe even have a little Calvados before Crystal and Nan finish the bottle." She got herself a glass.

"If you don't mind me joining you, would you grab a glass for me as well?"

She did and then poured them each a little brandy as Jean-Philippe put more logs in the fireplace to warm the room. She shut the bright overhead light, and they sat on the sofa, drinks in hand, the warmth and light of the fire casting a soothing glow over the room. She sipped some brandy and tried to calm her nerves.

Jean-Philippe remained silent.

"You made me curious," she began, "earlier, when you mentioned not having a place you think of as home. What did you mean?"

"I guess my childhood was an unusual one."

"Oh?" She took another sip of Calvados.

"Well, it's not really very interesting," he said after a while. "A scandal happened in my simple French family many years ago, and it changed everything for us. Some bad, some good. But the result was profound. I suspect it's why I've always felt unsettled."

"A scandal? That makes me curious," she admitted.

He studied the fire. "It was long ago, and hardly scandalous these days. But as to having a home, I may have given the wrong impression. It wasn't that I was homeless. Quite the opposite. I was pretty much raised by my grandmother. She was wealthy and brought me to beautiful spots all over the world. And we spent a lot of time living in hotels—fabulous hotels—but they weren't anything I'd call a home. As a result, my life has been unconventional, including my career choice. Recently, I decided it's time to act. And here I am."

Julia found the tale confusing and realized he had scarcely skimmed the surface. "And that's why you're in Idaho?"

"Hard to believe, isn't it?" He gave a small smile.

"And your being here involves my family?" she asked.

He looked momentarily surprised. "You figured that out, did you?"

"It wasn't exactly difficult," she admitted.

"Well, I don't know for sure that it does. Not yet," he said.

She was puzzled. "But—"

"It's a long story," he said abruptly, but then more softly added, "Not one for the middle of the night. Besides, I'd much rather hear about you."

"Me? Why?"

"For one thing," he hesitated, then said, "your reaction to your mother's song. You seemed unhappy to hear it, and I can't help but wonder why."

She sipped more brandy. "I can't—"

"Sometimes talking helps," he said softly, his eyes warm and open … and curious.

She hesitated. But then, maybe because she'd just heard her mother's voice after seventeen years, maybe because it was the middle of the night and she couldn't sleep, or maybe because he was a complete stranger who'd soon leave and she'd never see him again, something made her want to speak.

Still, she studied him to make sure he meant it when he said he wanted to hear her story. She saw no hint he'd been lying. She drew in her breath. "When I was four, my parents divorced and my father got full custody of me."

"Your father? That's rare in this country, isn't it?"

"Quite rare," she said.

His brows furrowed. "You were so young. It must have been difficult."

Her mind went back to those days that now made up her earliest memories. "It was. I don't remember specifically what happened. My parents would fight, but it didn't seem terribly serious. Then, one day, Roxanne was gone. She moved out, and it felt like a huge hole opened up in my life, a hole that would never be filled again."

"I can imagine," he said. "Do you have good memories of her, from before the divorce?"

She stared curiously at him. "It's strange, but no one else ever asked about those times. So long ago ... but I do remember how she would bring home little toys or candy for no good reason." And then she hesitated before saying, "I'm not even sure if it's a real memory or something I created in later years, but sometimes I think about hearing her voice when she sang. Even as a child playing in my room, I knew how beautiful it was." She shook her head, suddenly embarrassed. "I don't know why I'm telling you such things."

"Please, go on."

Memories rushed back at her. She leaned forward, and for some reason, spoke them aloud. "I also remember how my father changed after she left. So much joy was gone from our lives. I'll never forget the time I walked into his bedroom and saw him in tears. I ran up to him and tried to hug him. 'Daddy,' I said, but he pushed me away and said, 'Don't call me that.' I felt then that I'd lost both parents. Later, he apologized and held me close and said he loved me. But even as a child, I felt they were just words. And nothing was ever the same."

"I'm so sorry, Julia," he whispered.

"Don't be. It was a good lesson." She raised her chin. "It taught me that love can break your heart, and that there's nothing worse than watching the one you love walk away from you—either physically, or emotionally."

"That's too hard a lesson for a child," he said. "Did you see your mother after she left?"

"Each summer, Roxanne would invite me and my sisters to

spend a month with her here at the cabin. That was it. And those summer vacations with her ended when I was eighteen."

"Do you know why they ended?"

"No." She drew in her breath. "Rumor had it husband number four didn't want her spending time with 'other men's brats.' But I don't believe it. Roxanne wasn't one to take orders from anyone."

Jean-Philippe nodded. "Ah, something I suspect you share. But all that has made you who are today. I have the feeling you are a survivor, and strong. Someone who won't take any garbage from others. It's a good thing."

His words made her uncomfortable. She finished her drink, unused to receiving compliments. "That's me. One tough cookie," she said finally.

His eyes softened, and then he also finished his drink. To Julia's astonishment, he took their glasses and put them in the dishwasher. "Despite the strange, middle of the night circumstance," Jean-Philippe said, "I'm glad for our talk."

She liked hearing that. "Me, too," she admitted. "You go ahead upstairs. I'm going to double check the locks, then I'll be up."

"Okay. By the way, your hair, loose like that, is very beautiful. Its nearly white color makes it look as if you are surrounded by a cloud."

She was stunned into silence, then finally managed a quick, "Thank you."

"*Bon nuit, Julie.*"

She couldn't help but think how pretty her name sounded in French. She just stood there, feeling befuddled but oddly pleased, and didn't move until she heard his bedroom door shut.

CHAPTER 8

Julia breathed a sigh of relief. She'd survived her first breakfast with three lodgers to feed.

She had felt awkward when Jean-Philippe first showed up in the kitchen. He didn't say a word about the strange event in the middle of the night, or of their talk. He acted the same as always, and it gave her strength to do the same, although the charade couldn't bury the conversation they'd had or the memories they'd shared. Then, as he'd done the day before, he filled a thermos with coffee and quickly left.

As Julia cleaned up the kitchen, Crystal and Nan left the cabin. They said nothing about where they were going or anything else, which she guessed was usual for B&B guests. She didn't need to talk to them, and they didn't need to talk to her.

She freshened the bedrooms and the rest of the cabin since a bed and breakfast needed to be kept dust-free and spotless ... as opposed to her old apartment where some corners might have qualified for an archeological dig. She wondered if she would ever make enough money doing this to afford to hire help for the daily cleaning.

Julia was beyond pleased to see Lucas sitting on the log staring out at the water as she reached the riverbank. He turned as if aware of her presence before she reached him.

"Good afternoon," he called, hurrying to meet her. "You are carrying so much stuff! Can I help you?"

"Hello! Actually, you can." She handed him the closed box she carried. "This is a present for you."

"A present? No!"

"Yes."

She loved the joy on his face when he opened the box to find a foldable easel stand like hers, a canvas, palate, and oil paints. They had arrived the day before at the cabin. "I hope you like them."

"Like them? They're wonderful!" He looked amazed as she showed him how everything could be set up and ready to go. "This canvas is already stretched," he said with awe.

"It comes that way, silly," she said with a laugh. "Primed, too."

"Truly?" he asked. "This is too much."

"Not at all. From one artist to another. I'm glad to find someone else out here in Garden Valley who shares my interest."

He shook his head in astonishment at the supplies. "I am overwhelmed."

"What do you think you'll start with?" she asked.

"Well, what about a portrait of you?" he suggested.

"No way! I don't pose for one thing. I can't bear to remain still for many minutes on end. And painting me would be a waste of good paint! Besides, you must have some image in your head that you'd like to put on canvas. Many artists have that. Finally, here's your chance!"

He scarcely needed time to think. "You are right. There's something. Someone..."

"Who?" she asked, curious about the look in his eyes.

"I've always wanted a portrait of a woman I knew many years ago. I'll never forget what she looked like, but for a long time, I didn't want to paint her. And then, as I said, I lost interest, my paints dried up, and so on. But maybe I should paint her now, while I have the opportunity."

"She sounds important to you," Julia said. "You loved her, perhaps?"

He looked embarrassed. "Well, I'm sorry to say she was a married woman. A nurse, actually. She helped me while I was convalescing, and as far as I'm concerned, she saved my life. I don't think I would have made it without her."

"She sounds wonderful."

"She was," he whispered.

Her breath caught. "Was? She's passed away?"

"Oh, well ... I didn't mean it that way." He paused as if lost in thought, then asked, "Might I borrow a page from your sketch book? I'd like to sketch her before I attempt a painting."

She handed him the book. "Take it and use as many pages as you'd like. Here are my pencils. I rarely sketch before I paint."

"Thank you." He opened the book to a blank page, found a charcoal pencil, and began to draw. "We aren't in contact anymore, of course, which is why I used 'was.' It's also why I'd like to paint her portrait. Just to have something to remind me that the experience wasn't completely terrible."

She studied him. "How were you hurt?"

"During the war. A skirmish, I guess you'd call it. I was sent to the hospital for a gunshot to my leg when they realized the major problem was with my lungs. I went to a special ward for people with lungs like mine for complete rest. Thanks to good doctors, and the nurse I mentioned, I survived to come home."

"That's good! I can't imagine how awful that must have been for you to have your lungs damaged. I've heard stories of enemies in the Middle East using gas on their own people, so I guess I shouldn't be surprised that some gas reached our troops."

He frowned as he listened to her. "Of course," he murmured, keeping his eyes on the sketch book.

"Anyway, it's good you've got someone you want to paint," she added when he said nothing more. "It sounds like it's an idea you'll be able to put your heart into."

He smiled. "Definitely."

She noticed that, although he proclaimed the nurse was married, he didn't deny that he'd been in love with her. Poor fellow. It certainly helped explain why someone so relatively young and nice was alone in such a desolate area, and perhaps why he had such an air of sadness about him.

Of course, people could wonder the same about her, except that she hardly considered herself young anymore, and most people found her too caustic to call her "nice." And she wasn't sad. Not jolly, to be sure. But sad, no. Not her.

As she continued with her river scene, she noticed that Luke was fully engrossed in his sketch.

After a while, she glanced at her watch. It was one-thirty. She decided she should pack up and return to the cabin. It bothered her to have strangers lurking about and not be there.

"I'll get going," she said. "I have things to do at the cabin."

When his gaze lifted to meet hers, his eyes looked desolate and she couldn't help but think it had to do with the memories the sketch must have awakened in him. "Thank you for the paints." His voice was subdued. "You cannot imagine what they mean to me."

"I'm glad you like them." She gave him a gentle smile.

"Will you be here tomorrow?" he asked.

"I'll try my best."

He nodded, then said simply, "Good."

CHAPTER 9

After returning from the river, Julia spent the rest of the afternoon working on a logo, business cards, and a trifold brochure for the bed and breakfast. If no one wanted to hire her as a graphic designer, she would work for herself. She used the name "The Donnelly House," and as its logo she would make a simple pen-and-ink sketch of the cabin. Then, all she would need was to find a place to have the cards and brochures printed.

She was quite engrossed when Crystal and Nan bustled into the great room. "Idaho City is certainly tiny, isn't it? Nan, would you get me something cold to drink? I'm so worn out!" Crystal stated as she dropped into the easy chair by the fireplace, then faced Julia again. "I don't see how anyone is supposed to meet interesting men in a place so minuscule!"

"For such a thing to happen," Julia said archly, "would definitely be miraculous."

"Or supernatural," Nan said with a sly chuckle.

Julia shut her laptop. "I'll head upstairs. You two can relax down here. If you'd like to order a pizza, there's a place in

Garden Valley that will deliver. You can use the cabin's landline. Cell phones don't do too well in this area."

Just then Jean-Philippe entered the cabin. Julia felt as if the temperature in the room soared about ten degrees. She noticed Crystal and Nan sat up straighter and actually smiled. "You're already back," he said to his fellow guests as he removed his jacket and neck scarf and then headed to the kitchen to make himself a cup of coffee. "How did you find your travels?"

Julia kept her mouth shut as Crystal negatively compared small Idaho towns to historic, large, touristy places she'd been to. Jean-Philippe looked sorry he'd asked as Crystal droned on and on.

"So," Crystal said after she finished and no one asked her anything, "Nan and I are going to Mama's Folly for dinner. We hear that, for Crouch, they serve a decent meal."

"Their chicken-fried steak is a thing of beauty," Julia said.

"Why don't you come with us, Jean-Philippe?" Crystal suggested.

"Oh, well..." He looked stricken.

"Maybe Julia will come, too," Nan said with a small smile.

"Me?" Julia said. "I wouldn't want to impose on your vacation."

"You wouldn't be," Nan said. "You could tell us all about the area. And the menu."

"That sounds like a very good idea," Jean-Philippe added, his eyebrows high as he faced Julia.

"Well," Crystal frowned at Jean-Philippe's reaction to Julia joining them, but then she wriggled her shoulders. "I suppose you should come along, Julia, unless you have other dinner plans. It'll be my treat."

"I couldn't do that," Julia said.

"Of course, you could." Crystal ran a fingertip over an eyebrow, suddenly seeming to relish the role of Lady Bountiful as her gaze swept over Julia's baggy clothes. "I insist. I'll even drive. Want to ride with us, Jean-Philippe?"

"I'll follow," he said.

"Guess we're all going," Julia said uneasily.

"Do we need to dress up?" Nan asked.

Julia couldn't help but smile. "In a word, no."

Julia, Jean-Philippe, and Crystal all ordered what was billed as "Mama's famous" chicken-fried steak with mashed potatoes and gravy. Nan chose Idaho finger steaks—breaded, deep-fried pieces of tenderloin served with a horseradish cocktail sauce.

They were seated in the restaurant section, but the country-western band was easy to hear, as was the applause from people watching and dancing to the music. Julia soon stopped paying attention to Crystal's constant chatter and looked around at the other customers.

Her gaze turned to one who seemed somehow familiar. He was a tall, broad-shouldered fellow with curly brown hair and dark eyes, standing with other men near the bar. They were drinking beers and looking at the dancers.

Then, she remembered. Nathan Zabinski. She'd run into him briefly last year when she was overseeing the cabin's remodel. He was close friends with Mallory's boyfriend, Gunnar McDermott.

Nathan was one of the kids that Julia's younger sisters used to play with during the girls' summer month at the cabin. Remembering those days was always bittersweet for Julia, and her middle of the night conversation with Jean-Philippe had brought many memories back to her.

The summer she'd turned five, after her parents had been divorced for a year, Roxanne had invited Julia to join her at the

Donnelly family cabin for a month—just as they'd spent past Julys there—only this time, her father wouldn't be joining them. Still, Julia had been thrilled at the thought of seeing her mom again. But when she arrived, she found that Roxanne had a new husband and a new baby. When Julia watched Roxanne with Carly, she saw what mother love should look like. She never remembered Roxanne gushing over her that way.

Little Julia had been fiercely jealous of Carly. For a while that jealousy turned to hate for her mother and the baby which resulted in her acting out quite a bit and getting into lots of trouble with Roxanne. But then, five years later, the scenario repeated itself. That time, she saw the disappointment and the hurt on Carly's face when Roxanne showed up with her latest offspring, their sister Mallory.

Julia had felt pity for Carly and finally started to treat her little sister decently. But the two never grew close.

Julia couldn't help but wonder how long Roxanne's third marriage would last. She found out the summer Mallory turned six years old. Roxanne and her third husband had separated, and Mallory had been devastated.

Julia hated the way Roxanne had walked out on her and her father and what it had done to them, but her hatred had turned visceral when she saw the effects on her little sisters. They were sweet little girls. How could Roxanne not see that?

As Julia grew older, she had also questioned why Roxanne would spend a month each year in Garden Valley? Why had she wanted her daughters with her? And especially, why didn't she want them the other eleven months of the year? What was so special about July?

And even worse, why did she go from one man to another? Julia knew that when Roxanne died, she was alone. So why was she never happy with any of her husbands? What was she looking for that she never found? At times, Julia wondered if there wasn't a lost love out there somewhere. Considering that Roxanne's ex's were all nice enough men, she thought "the one that got away"—if that was what had happened—must have been amazing: incredibly handsome, filthy rich, and maybe involved in stage or screen. Losing a man like that, she could see, would have made Roxanne quite unhappy.

But Julia never asked, and Roxanne never said. And now she was gone. Julia knew no one who could answer those questions for her.

"That was so good!" The change in Crystal's voice interrupted Julia's lengthy walk down memory lane. "I think I'll have coffee and a yummy dessert."

"You might want to wait on that," Julia said.

"I don't think so!" Crystal announced.

"Well, you ladies are here to meet some fellows, right? I see one that I know, and he's talking with a couple of other guys. Why don't we order an after-dinner drink from the bar and I'll introduce you to him?"

"Oh? I like that idea." Crystal stood up.

"I don't think so," Nan said. "I'll wait right here."

"No, you won't." Julia tugged at her hand and pulled her from her chair. "We're just going get a drink and say hello. Nothing more. I'm not saying you need to marry them or even to dance with them, but you've got to at least say hello to some single men while you're here."

"*Pardon?*" Jean-Philippe pretended to be hurt.

The three women laughed. "Besides your handsome fellow lodger, that is," Julia said, smiling at him.

"I will join you," he said as he also got to his feet and took Julia's arm. "But it's not to meet your cowboy friends."

She guessed as much. She'd already noticed a lot of young, attractive women smiling at him, and probably wondering what such a handsome guy was doing with Crystal, Nan, and her.

Julia walked her lodgers through the restaurant and then skirted the dance floor to the bar where they gave their orders. Drinks in hand, she headed for Nathan, the three following like ducklings with their mother.

"Nathan Zabinski, is that you?" she said.

His back was to her, and he turned. "Oh, my God! Julia Perrin!" Suddenly he put his hands up as if he were being arrested. "I didn't do it! Honest!"

She laughed. She knew where that was coming from. "Of course you did! You were always guilty of something."

"Yeah, I guess you're right. Good to see you again!" His mouth upturned into a big smile that reached his eyes as he gave her what amounted to a bear hug, given how big he was to Julia's small frame. Julia had never been a hugger and usually hated it, but she welcomed his attempt and smiled broadly. "I heard you're living at the cabin now," he added.

"I am. The Donnelly House bed and breakfast. And these are my lodgers, Crystal, Nan, and … hmm, the third one has disappeared for the moment." She looked around and saw that Jean-Philippe was surrounded by three women who were jabbering and looking at him with something akin to worship. She shook her head and turned back to Crystal and Nan. "This is an old friend, Nathan."

They said hello and then the two men Nathan had been talking to stepped up and introduced themselves as Deon and Shane. Deon was broad shouldered and muscular, while Shane was smaller, but also well-toned. The move was subtle, but Julia noticed Nathan side-step as if to distance himself from the other two. She did the same.

"Where are you gals from?" Deon asked, eying Crystal. His face was well-tanned and lined from harsh, dry weather, but the darkness only emphasized the blue of his eyes, while Shane's face was ruddier, more sun-burnt than tanned. Deon and Shane wore not-too-wide brimmed brown cowboy hats, typical Idaho attire, but Crystal and Nan gawked at the men and their hats as if they were some strange alien creatures. Julia also noticed that both Deon and Shane looked older than Nathan, probably in their forties, and didn't wear wedding rings.

"We're from Chicago," Crystal said.

"What brings you to Idaho?" Deon asked, flashing her a cocky smile.

She looked pleasantly surprised. "Just want to see this part of the country," she replied.

"And just how're you finding it, sweet thing?"

She coyly gazed long at him. "Better by the minute, handsome."

"Is that so?" Deon's eyebrows went up, and he sidled closer to Crystal.

Julia felt her dinner start to rise in her throat and had to stop paying attention to those two. She turned to Nathan. "What are you up to these days?"

He took a few more steps away from the odd foursome. "I'm working at Gunnar's auto repair shop for now."

"Oh, nice." Mallory had told Julia all about Gunnar's auto repair business, and that he often gave work to vets who were having some difficulties adjusting to civilian life.

A simple line dance started to "Louisiana Saturday Night," which wasn't too fast, but had a strong beat. A lot of people hurried out to the dance floor. "Let's join in," Nathan said. "It's fun, and I know you can line dance, Julia. I remember you showing me, Gunnar, and your sisters some steps."

She grimaced. "Not by choice!" It had been a Roxanne brainstorm to make Julia teach the younger kids, then at places like Mama's or at town picnics, she would get out on the dance floor with them all in a row as if they were the Trapp Family or something, and they'd all dance in sync. Julia wouldn't have been surprised if Roxanne began belting out that the hills were alive with the sound of music! Mercifully, she never did.

"It was a hoot," Nathan said with a grin.

"Spare me," Julia said, then hooked Nan's arm. "Let's go. Shane? Do you line dance?"

"No way." He rushed off to get another drink.

"But Crystal..." Nan protested.

Crystal was in deep conversation with Deon. "She looks busy," Julia said.

"I've never done this." Nan looked worried.

"I'll show you. You can do it," Julia said.

Nan had no idea what to do, but Julia stuck with her and by the third time through, she was starting to pick up the steps. Finally, Julia was thrilled to hear the serious young woman actually laugh out loud when she found that she'd turned left while everyone else turned right, and she ended up staring at the dancers all heading her way.

When the song ended and they walked off the dance floor, Nan had her hands on her cheeks. "Oh, my! I've never done anything like that. It was crazy."

"But fun?" Julia asked.

"Oh, yes!"

They went back to the bar area. "Well, I put in overtime this morning, so I'm plenty tired," Nathan said. "I'm going to call it a night."

"I ought to be going, too," Julia said to Nan. "I wonder if we can get Crystal away from Deon."

"I would suggest you do," Nathan said quietly as he was leaving. "I just don't know about that guy."

"Got it." Julia nodded. "Nan, would you tell Crystal we're ready to head back to the cabin?"

"I don't know if she wants to be interrupted," Nan said nervously.

Julia looked around. "I don't see Jean-Philippe, so either Crystal drives us, or we start walking. And this area has bears."

Crystal didn't look happy at Nan's interruption, but she soon joined Julia.

"This was a most interesting evening," Crystal said with a big smile. She drove them back to the cabin carrying on the whole way about what a neat fellow Deon Simms was, and how he worked at a cattle ranch just north of Garden Valley. The way she talked, that was the most interesting and challenging occupation she'd ever heard of.

Julia was curled up on the sofa, book in hand, when Jean-Philippe entered the cabin. "Hello," she said, being unsure what more to say considering she last saw him with a virtual harem. To ask if he had had fun sounded way too nosy.

It was close to freezing outside, and he was bundled in a heavy jacket and a long plaid scarf. He took them off and stood near the fireplace, holding his hands out to warm them. "It looked like you met a good friend at Mama's," he said. "A close friend."

"Yes. He used to play with my little sisters. I sometimes babysat all of them and apparently scared the bejeezus out of him."

Jean-Philippe eyebrows lifted. "Oh. I see. So, you two are not..."

She grimaced. "Good God, no."

He frowned uncertainly. "Still, you and the ladies looked like you were having fun talking and dancing."

"It was fun, much to my surprise," she admitted. "I haven't line danced since I was a teenager. That was an old song I used to dance to, and I was surprised at how quickly the steps came back to me. Have you ever tried line dancing?"

He rubbed his temple. "I don't know if these French feet could do it."

She chuckled. "Sure they can."

"Do I need cowboy boots?"

"We can get you some of those as well. And you definitely need some blue jeans around here."

He chuckled. "*Mon Dieu!*"

"You said it!" She couldn't help but laugh.

He smiled back at her. "Next time we go there perhaps you will show me how to do this line dance?"

Her breath caught. Was he asking for a date? No. Obviously not. "Why didn't you try it tonight? I'm sure at least one of the ladies you were with would have gladly given you instructions." Her voice sounded harsher than she'd intended.

His pale eyes studied her a long moment before he said, "Because I had no interest in dancing with them. Or anything else."

She picked up what he was saying but didn't know how to react. She wasn't a woman used to bantering with men. So, she turned back to the pages of her book as she muttered, "Okay, then. I'll show you … next time."

"Good." He took a step toward her, but then stopped. "I'll say goodnight now. I won't disturb you further."

You aren't disturbing me, she wanted to say, but instead she simply nodded and with eyes glued to words that could have been written in Swahili for all the sense they now made to her, whispered, "Goodnight."

CHAPTER 10

Julia decided to make pancakes to go with the eggs, bacon, sausage, and all the fruit, yogurt, and cereal that Carly had insisted any good B&B should put out for breakfast even if no one ate them.

Crystal and Nan didn't show up for breakfast until nine a.m. and only wanted pancakes with their coffee which was good since Julia had mixed too much pancake batter because she'd been thinking so intently about Jean-Philippe's suggestion that they go to Mama's Folly. Of course it wasn't a date, it being the only place in town to get a big meal. But it made her think about the dates she'd had. She'd dated in college, but whenever one of her boyfriends started to get close—emotionally close—she broke it off. One of them said she was scared of falling in love. No, she wasn't scared. She just didn't believe in the emotion. Lust, sure—that was easy. But love? Hah!

After leaving college, her few dates had turned out awful. Somewhere around age thirty—some five years ago—she gave up on the whole idea of "sharing" her life with anyone. Some people were better off alone, and she was one of them.

She could hardly sleep last night wondering what a happy loner like her had suddenly gotten herself into running a place like this. For one thing, she should have refused to go to Mama's with any of her lodgers, male or female. That was mixing business with pleasure, and not something she should have done.

On the other hand, it had been Friday night, so why shouldn't she have gone? She wasn't *that* old and did she really need to spend all her Friday and Saturday nights home alone? And it had actually been an enjoyable evening. Besides, who knew what mischief Crystal might have gotten herself into if she hadn't been there?

As soon as Crystal finished her stack of pancakes, she told Julia that she had invited Deon and Shane to come to the cabin for pizzas at lunchtime. Julia was horrified. At the same time, Jean-Philippe came downstairs, mumbled a sleepy "good morning," and headed for the coffee.

Crystal's voice cut through the house like a buzz saw. "Also, Julia, I'd like you to help me set up everything for my company? I do hope you have enough clean glasses and plates and silverware. After all, you did say 'mi casa es su casa.'"

Julia's mouth dropped. "Uh, well, I'm sure—"

Jean-Philippe cut in. "Or, if you aren't busy here, Julia, I'm going to the forest today to check on my equipment. Perhaps you'd like to come along?"

Her mouth dropped with surprise. Had she been that obvious in her dislike of Crystal's suggestion, as well as her guests? *Yes!* She wanted to say. But she thought of those two oafs coming to the cabin, using her dishes, and such, made her decide she should keep an eye on everyone. "Looks like I'm busy," she blurted.

"Okay." He nodded, picked up his thermos and left before she even had a chance to give him some food to take with him.

Her heart sank as she watched him head out the door without her.

———

Crystal's invitees were about fifteen minutes late, which meant that Julia had to put up with her fretting that she was going to be stood up. "They'll be here," Julia said.

The pizza arrived about ten minutes after Deon and Shane did. Julia had rushed to the store for paper plates and plastic utensils, and even plastic beer cups, put them out on the kitchen counter to Crystal's clear disdain, and then left the downstairs to her guests and their dates.

She did, however, keep the bedroom door ajar so she could hear if anything went amiss.

Deon immediately began talking about his adventures on the Payette and other rivers in Idaho, how some of them were category five rapids at certain times of year, and that the rivers could be quite dangerous for anyone who didn't know what they were doing.

Julia finally could take no more of Crystal's oohs and aahs as Deon pontificated and Nan and Shane remained silent. She shut her door and went to work on the cabin's website.

An hour later, she heard a knock on the door. She groaned, imagining it was Crystal wanting her to do something for the "party."

She opened the door to find Jean-Philippe. His eyes crinkled with a smile as he said, "I've come to rescue you."

She could have kissed him.

———

Jean-Philippe was happy to see Julia's delight at his appearing at her door. "There were enough people out at the forest today that they didn't need me," he explained. "So I came back here. You don't need to hide out in your room. And, since I know you are Miss Practical, you mentioned needing to go to a print shop. Why don't we find one for you?"

Her smile of surprise broadened, and he couldn't help but notice how pretty she was when she smiled—and that she didn't do it nearly often enough.

"The only problem is there might not be one in town," she said.

"We'll find out. And we can always go to Boise. As you told Crystal, it's not that far away. So, let's give it a try. All work and no play is no good for anyone. This way, we can combine the two."

She gathered up her laptop and the mockups she'd printed of the brochure and business cards. As Jean-Philippe drove her into Crouch, she searched on her phone for a print shop.

"There are several in Boise," she said. "Or, if you'd like to head north, there's a commercial print shop in Cascade, about an hour north, or we can go another half-hour to McCall."

He nodded. "Let's head north for a change. We can try Cascade, and if it doesn't work, it's on to McCall."

Jean-Philippe was happy to make the drive that followed the main stem of the Payette River north through the mountains. As he drove his truck, he entertained Julia with stories of traveling to a number of different countries with his grandmother, who he called "Grandmere." Some stories were humorous, some poignant. Julia seemed to enjoy them. For that, he was glad.

When they reached the town of Cascade, the print shop was just off the highway. "Here we are," he said.

"This shouldn't take long." She gathered her things. "And

afterward, maybe we should go up to McCall and you can see Payette Lake—the source of the river."

They entered the shop and in a moment a man stepped out of the backroom. He was fairly short with hair that looked almost white. He froze as he looked at them, then proceeded behind the counter. "Can I help you?"

Jean-Philippe noticed that while some of the proprietor's hair was white with age, most of it was light blond, a shade similar to Julia's. And the man's eyes, like Julia's, were a greenish-blue color.

"I need some business cards and a brochure printed up," Julia said. She placed her mock-ups on the counter.

The man stared at her a moment before he picked up the brochure with its pictures of the inside and out of the cabin. He looked it over. "I'm sure we can do these easily." His voice quavered slightly.

Jean-Philippe kept watching the shop owner and sensed a strange undercurrent as the man now discussed the number of copies Julia wanted printed and the cost. He seemed to spend more time looking at her than at the material she was giving him.

"I see you brought your laptop." The proprietor handed Julia a USB stick. "You'll get a better result if you transfer your files to this thumb drive."

"Great. I was hoping you'd say that." She put the thumb drive in her computer and found the files and quickly transferred them. "I put the files under my name, Julia Perrin."

As the proprietor took back the drive, his eyes searched her face. "Yes. All right." His voice was scarcely a whisper.

Just then, the shop's door burst open and a teenage boy entered. "Oops," he mumbled seeing Julia and Jean-Philippe. "Didn't mean to disturb you." The boy had silky whitish blond hair, a slight frame, and a big smile. His blue eyes with dark brows and long lashes surrounding them were striking. Jean-Philippe's mouth dropped as he gaped from the boy to the print shop owner to Julia and back.

"Dad, can I borrow the car? I need to go up to McCall for a couple hours."

Julia stared at the teenager, a quizzical look on her face.

The proprietor reached into his pocket for the car keys. "Be careful, and I expect you back by four."

"Thanks." He took the keys and left.

The proprietor stared after him with a grimace. "He just got his driver's license. Constantly finds a reason to drive." He then took a form, wrote down the number of items to be printed and his estimate, signed his name—Miika Halkonen—and handed it to Julia. "You'll need to fill the top out. It'll take a couple days. I'll call you when it's done."

"Sounds good," she said as she wrote down her name, address, and phone number, and then signed the form.

"Miika Halkonen," Jean-Philippe said. "Are you Finnish?"

"Yeah, but everyone calls me Mike," the proprietor said. "And you sound French."

"I am. Have you been in this country long?"

"Since I was a baby," Halkonen said.

"It seems to be a good place to grow up. Now I understand your very light blond hair," Jean-Philippe said.

Halkonen's eyes darted to Julia's hair, then he stared hard at Jean-Philippe and squared his shoulders. "My hair is white. I'm old." He folded his copy of the authorization form. "As I said, I'll call when the print job is finished."

As they were about to walk out of the store, Jean-Philippe took Julia's arm, but then turned to the shop owner. "Just wondering, the cabin in the brochure belonged to the Donnelly family. Did you know Roxanne Donnelly? She was quite well known around here."

A long moment passed. "Of course I've heard of her." Halkonen's jaw was tight. "I knew her, a bit. Do you ... do you know how she is? Or where?"

Jean-Philippe faced Julia who drew in her breath and then said, "I'm sorry to say, she passed away last year."

The proprietor's face drained of all color. "I hadn't heard," he whispered. "Excuse me." As he turned to go into the back room, his hand reached for the door frame as if to steady himself.

Julia and Jean-Philippe looked at each other as they left the shop. "Poor man," Julia murmured. "It seems he must have known Roxanne better than he let on."

Jean-Philippe was tempted to say more, but then thought better of it. In the end, he only said, "So it seems."

CHAPTER 11

Relief filled Julia that Deon and Shane's green Ford F-150 truck was gone when she and Jean-Philippe returned to the cabin. But when she opened the door, she heard Crystal screeching like a banshee. Nan stood clutching the bannister halfway down the stairs, looking too scared to continue either up or down.

"What's going on?" Julia yelled over the screams, rushing into the great room to see Crystal running in circles.

"Stop him!" Crystal cried.

Jean-Philippe looked at Julia and shook his head, mystified.

"Stop who? No one is here," Julia said.

Crystal grabbed Julia and in her hurry to get behind the small woman, nearly lifted her off her feet as she spun her around, placing Julia between her and whatever she feared was pursuing her.

"What are you doing?" Julia struggled to free herself from Crystal's grip.

"Miss Crystal," Jean-Philippe said, taking hold of Crystal's arm, "please, let Julia go. You are hurting her, and nothing is after you."

"You're wrong." Crystal let Julia go but then catapulted into Jean-Philippe's arms, nearly bowling him over. "I was being chased. It was a mouse!"

"A mouse?" Julia cried. "You're carrying on like this because of a mouse? We are in the country, you know. There are mice all over! And we've got two cats, so if a mouse got into this cabin, it won't bother anyone very long." She looked around. Neither cat was in sight.

"But the mouse was already dead." Crystal let go of Jean-Philippe and swallowed hard. "It was flat and lifeless and then it suddenly rose up and dangled in front of my face. I jumped away from it, but it came after me. And it wouldn't let me go upstairs to my room and lock the door. Whenever I'd get near the stairs, it jumped between me and them. It was the most horrible thing I've ever experienced."

"If there ever was such a clever-but-dead mouse," Julia said, "where is it now?"

"How should I know?" Crystal shrieked.

"I know," Jean-Philippe said, standing behind an easy chair. "Do you have a broom and dust-pan, Julia? I'll get rid of it for you. It's most certainly dead."

Hearing his words, Crystal stormed to the stairs. "I don't know what's going on here, all I know is, I've never been so frightened in my life. I just may sue!"

Julia rushed to the foyer after her. "Sue? And tell the judge a dead mouse levitated and chased you? Good luck with that."

Crystal reached the top of the stairs and looked back down at her. "I'm leaving, and since this is how you treat your guests, I'm not paying you one cent! Good luck with *that!*" She stomped up into her room and slammed the door so hard the entire cabin shook.

"Great," Julia said to Jean-Philippe. "Now what am I supposed to do?"

"Can you run her credit card?"

"She can stop payment. And it'll probably be more trouble and bad publicity than it's worth if she wanted to pursue what a crazy place this is. Not to mention the ghosts that supposedly live here. She could go after me saying I'm perpetrating a scam on the public. No, it's best to just let her go."

"This could be her way of getting out of paying," Jean-Philippe said.

"Frankly, I think she let herself grow hysterical and imagined the whole thing. At least the mouse is dead."

"Yes. The broom..."

Julia found a broom and dustpan, and Jean-Philippe took care of getting the mouse carcass out of the house.

She sat in the great room and watched as Crystal and Nan walked out the door. Nan gave her a quick look filled with sadness but, as usual, she didn't say a word.

Jean-Philippe had to admit he felt sorry that Julia had to go through this. He could tell how uncomfortable people made her to begin with, and Crystal was the type that would be a trial for anyone. The usually firm and hard-nosed innkeeper looked as if she'd just been through hell and back. Her reaction when she learned he'd be staying here for a number of days told him money must be tight, and now, Crystal not paying, had to be a blow.

Still, as ridiculous as the situation with Crystal was, what had happened at the print shop was even stranger.

He had no idea if Julia simply didn't recognize the fact, or if she wouldn't allow herself to acknowledge that she, the print shop owner, and his son bore a startlingly strong resemblance to each other. His mind whirred with the possible reasons.

From the moment the shopkeeper had stared at Julia when he first saw her, to his reaction when he learned of Roxanne's death, gave Jean-Philippe a good idea of what was going on there. But if Julia didn't see it, it certainly wasn't his place to tell her. Particularly not while she refused to allow him or, apparently, anyone else to get close to her.

He thought of her late night tale about her mother walking out and her father rejecting her when she caught him crying—and now, her father pushing her and saying not to call him 'Daddy' took on added significance. He could understand any child having trouble with that, and Julia ran deep. He hoped he was leaping to conclusions that weren't there.

"It'll be all right," he said and sat beside her on the sofa. He knew he was a being very un-twenty-first century, but he suddenly felt protective of her.

"I can imagine what my sisters will say." She bowed her head, folding her arms tight. "My second guest has threatened to sue me. Great!"

"What do you think was really going on here with that mouse?" he asked, but the words were no sooner out of his mouth than the image of Crystal running about the house being "chased" by a dead mouse popped into his head. A tiny snicker escaped from his throat and it was all he could do to keep a straight face.

"Are you laughing about this?" She spun toward him, angry.

"I'm sorry," he said, struggling to hold back. "But I never knew anyone could make such sounds." He burst into laughter.

"It's not funny!"

He laughed harder. "And she was running so fast, she could have made an Olympics team."

Julia tried not to join him, but before long, she was laughing so hard she had tears in her eyes.

"I'm glad to see you laugh," he told her when he could breathe again. He vowed to help her find ways to laugh more often.

"You're terrible!" She wiped her eyes. "It's your fault I'm not feeling sorry for that poor woman!"

"Very terrible, I know." With any other woman, he would have taken her in his arms after sharing a crazy moment like that, and he had a good idea where it would have led. But not with this one. He stood. "So, I will make it up to you. Go upstairs, rest, and I'm going to cook dinner for us. Okay?"

"You're *what?*" She looked as if she hadn't heard right.

"You heard me. Now go. I'm going to the store, and when I get back, no peeking."

A couple of hours later, he was pleased by the sight and aroma of the dinner. He'd made *coq au vin*—chicken cooked in red wine with carrots, onions, mushrooms, to which he also added a little bacon, brandy, butter, and lots of seasonings. With it he served roasted potatoes and a green salad. And, of course, red wine to wash it down. He even put a candle on the table.

He called Julia to join him.

Her expression as she approached the dinner table was everything he'd hoped for. "It all looks so delicious!" Julia gasped. "I can't believe I was praising Mama's food and taking you there, when you can cook like this!"

"I'm French, remember?" he said. "But I'm afraid the 'French' bread here isn't very good. Someday I'll bake the real thing for you."

He dished out, and when she tasted the chicken, she was even more impressed.

They ate in silence for a while. She asked, "So what is the job you're doing out in the Boise forest?"

He took a sip of wine. "I'm looking for falcon smugglers."

"Did you say smugglers?" she asked as if she hadn't heard him right.

"It's a long story," he said. "As I've mentioned, my specialty is the study of raptors. Well, one winter I went with Grandmere to Dubai and we were invited out to the desert with some very rich sheiks. I discovered that falconry—hunting with falcons— was very popular throughout the region. People are spending huge amounts for a bird, or a falcon's eggs. As a result, smuggling has become a problem."

"People really smuggle birds?" She looked surprised.

"Absolutely. And one of the most valuable falcons is the gyrfalcon. It's the largest falcon. Incredible, beautiful birds, usually white and gray. They live in the arctic, but in winter many fly south to try to find food—including to Idaho. That's when smugglers get involved."

"You're kidding."

"Ah, I see that you have finished your dinner. Let me clear the table for you."

Julia helped him to both clear the table and then clean up the kitchen. As Jean-Philippe washed and she dried, he continued his story. "Evidence exists that some smugglers are operating north of Garden Valley in the Boise National Forest. The Peregrine Foundation which is dedicated to the preservation of endangered birds and headquartered in Boise asked me to become a part of a team of scientists and law enforcement to do what we can to find and stop them."

She gaped. "Really? How interesting."

"What's going on is bad, Julia. The local smugglers are hoping to capture a rare gyrfalcon in their nets—they're worth tens of thousands of dollars. But they're also trapping the more abundant peregrine falcons. Even peregrines bring in several thousands on the black market."

"It's sad what people will do for money," she said with a shake of the head.

"It's also evil," he added.

"I agree."

Their work in the kitchen done, Jean-Philippe made them each a cup of coffee and poured snifters of brandy.

They moved to the sofa in front of the fire.

Finally, he asked the question he'd been wanting to ask ever since he'd gotten to know Julia. "So, tell me, Miss Julia Perrin, why are you still single? I'm surprised one of these cowboys hasn't put a ring on your finger."

She shook her head. "No way."

"Have you ever come close?"

She shook her head. "There was never anyone special, I'm afraid."

"No?"

After a moment she said, "I dated when I was a dumb teenager, but more to defy my father than anything. And then I found out he didn't care what I did. He even left me and took off for Australia when I was a senior in high school. Five hundred bucks and a 'see ya later, kid.' That was fun. Luckily a girlfriend's mom took me in until I graduated." She shrugged. "Not until college did I realize I'd rather stay home than go to parties where people acted stupid. Love seemed overrated."

A moment of silence went by. "And now, are you happy?"

"Content," she replied, her voice flat.

"I see," he murmured with a slow nod.

They sat in silence for a while, then she asked, "What about you? Have you been married?"

He leaned back against the sofa. "Grandmere was always finding women she thought I should date. They were always beautiful, accomplished, and well-educated, but for some reason, it never worked out. I felt, I don't know, that something was missing. That there should be something more, if that makes sense."

"What did your Grandmere say about that?"

"She said when I found the right woman, I'd know it. But she also used to worry that I would be lonely when she was gone." His voice softened. "What was always amusing to me was that the women she kept wanting me to meet were quite different from her. I couldn't help but suspect that was the problem with them."

"What do you mean?"

The memories brought a smile to his face. "Grandmere was self-taught which is why she placed such a value on education. And although she was just a little thing, she was strong and feisty. And fearless. And adventurous. No one could put anything over on her. But despite how tough and uncompromising the world thought she was, inside, her heart was big. She was very special to me."

Julia smiled. "You were lucky to have someone like that in your life. Someone to look up to."

"I was," he murmured, then stood. "And now, I am completely on my own. I can go where I want, when I want. It's one of the benefits of my line of work—and having inherited from Grandmere."

"Where are you going next?"

"I haven't decided. I've been offered research positions in Spain and in Greenland—quite a difference, isn't it? I'm not sure which is more interesting. The work in Greenland is, but then Spain—who wouldn't want to spend time there?"

She nodded. "I can imagine. You're lucky."

"Yes, I would say so."

"You asked me, so I'll ask you the same question, are you happy?"

He gave a very Gallic one-shouldered shrug. "What is happiness? But I can see the world, so I'm not complaining."

"I should think not!" she said.

He smiled. "Well, I have 'bent your ear,' as they say, long enough. I should say goodnight. I must rise early and go to the forest in the morning to relieve the night watchman there."

Worry crossed her face. "I hope it isn't dangerous."

"Only if we see the smugglers—and they see us. We're being very careful."

Her gaze captured his. "You've asked me in the past if I'd like to go with you to the forest. I said no because I was busy, but next time you ask, I'll say yes."

He was surprised and oddly touched by her statement. "That will be soon," he said.

She smiled. "Good. And thank you for tonight. I really enjoyed the dinner and the conversation."

"Me, too, *Julie. Bon nuit.*"

"*Bon nuit.*"

CHAPTER 12

J ean-Philippe was gone before Julia even got up the
following morning. After a while, she grabbed her easel
and paints and hurried down to the spot by the river
where she and Luke usually met. He wasn't there.

Distant mountains showed the snow line creeping ever
lower, and soon it would blanket her little valley. She wore a
heavy jacket and put the hood up, covering her head against the
cold, and then sat on the ground leaning back against the felled
log. More than painting, she wanted a moment of relaxation.
Shutting her eyes, she listened to the lapping of the river water
hitting the rocks, an occasional cry of a hawk or osprey, and the
rustle of leaves under a gentle wind. The light scent of earth and
river filled her senses. Not so long ago, in her city apartment,
the smell of gasoline and diesel was constant. She'd gotten used
to it, but now she knew what clean air smelled like and couldn't
imagine going back.

Although the air was crisp, the sun felt warm. She felt herself
relaxing, finally.

"Are you asleep?"

She recognized Luke's voice even as he whispered. "I don't think I'm sleeping."

"Or if you were, I just woke you up, right? And now I'm in trouble?" He sat down on the log.

She joined him, sitting on the log. "I didn't make it here yesterday because one of my lodgers decided to hold a party. I tried to stay and oversee the cabin, but it was too awful. I just couldn't take all that joviality."

He chuckled. "I understand the feeling. I'm not much for 'joviality' either."

"You're making fun of me," she said.

"Not at all." He lost his smile and turned more serious. "Were they there because of the ghost stories about the cabin? I mean, female lodgers, inviting some young men over ... you know what it sounds like."

She stared at him. "How did you know my lodgers are female, or they invited men over?"

He shrugged. "Am I wrong?"

"No. But still, how did you know?"

He tapped his temple with his forefinger, not answering.

"Fine," she said. She didn't want to argue with him, although dating sites like Match-dot-com proved men were just as likely as women to use many means to seek out the right woman. But she decided to let it go.

"So, what are they doing now at the cabin, these guests of yours?"

"They're gone, just like that." She snapped her fingers and couldn't help but smile.

"You don't look like you mind."

"I don't! Only that they didn't pay, but at least I've got another lodger."

An eyebrow lifted. "Something in your tone tells me it's fine if *he* stays."

She frowned. "How did you know it's a 'he'?"

"I told you, something in your tone," he said with a small smile.

She shook her head. "I have no idea what you're talking about. And besides, while you seem to know so much about me and the cabin, I don't even know your last name."

"Didn't I tell it to you? Oh, look at that bird." He stood and pointed to a tall fir. "At the very top. It's a falcon, almost white. I wonder if it's one of those arctic birds that come here. They're very rare."

She stood and looked where he pointed. In a moment, the bird took flight. "Oh, my! It's beautiful. Look at how high it soars and so fast. Yet, it's obviously hunting for food on the ground. What must it be like to have such eyesight?"

Luke nodded. "There are wonders in this world that are stranger than anything the human mind can conceive," he murmured, giving her an enigmatic look. "Man is so proud, yet he knows so very little about the forces that surround him."

"You're right about that," she murmured, then glanced at her watch. "My goodness! I must have fallen asleep. The afternoon is all but gone."

"Before I forget, here's your sketch book." He handed her the tablet. "I don't need my drawing any longer. I've captured it on the canvas. Now I have to work with colors to get them right."

"Are you sure?" she asked.

"I am. But I might borrow it again one of these days to do another sketch. One of you, perhaps."

She shook her head. "I already told you, I'm not portrait worthy."

"You're wrong." He backed away. "See you tomorrow, I hope."

"Me, too," she said, then turned her steps toward the cabin.

Jean-Philippe didn't return to the cabin until nearly two a.m., long after Julia had retired for the night. The next morning, she let herself sleep in, sure Jean-Philippe would do the same. She could hardly wait to see the expression on his face when she told him she'd actually seen a gyrfalcon right near the cabin. She could scarcely believe her luck.

But when she finally got up, dressed, and went downstairs, she found Jean-Philippe sitting by the fireplace, her sketchbook in hand. His head jerked up at the sound of her footsteps, and his expression was a mishmash of confusion, anger, and something akin to fear.

She didn't understand and immediately became defensive about the amateurish sketches that were in the book. "You shouldn't look at those." She wanted to snatch the sketch book away and walked over to him. "They're just quick drawings. I can do better, believe me."

"That's not it, I—"

"I drew most of those long ago," she explained. "But lately, I've felt like painting again. That's the only reason my sketch book is out. Just give it to me."

He jumped to his feet. "Julia, stop. All I want is for you to explain this." He turned the sketch pad around, his eyes hard. "Did you draw it?"

It was the sketch Luke did of his nurse. Why was Jean-Philippe so troubled by it? "No. I lent the book to a neighbor. He did it."

A strange look came over Jean-Philippe's face. "A neighbor?"

"We meet at the river and enjoy painting."

He shook his head and paced before he spun and faced her. After a long moment he asked, "Is your neighbor very old, by chance?"

"Not at all. Probably younger than me." She was taken aback by Jean-Philippe's intensity.

"*Why did he draw such a portrait?*" he demanded.

She went to the sofa, sat, and waited a moment to give him time to calm down. "He was in the military, and when he needed medical care, the woman he drew was his nurse."

Jean-Philippe gasped, his expression incredulous.

"When?" The word was little more than a whisper.

"When? I have no idea."

"Which country was he in when he met this nurse?" Jean-Philippe asked.

"Jean-Philippe, why is this so important to you? I hardly know the man and you're asking me about his life story."

He said nothing and waited. She added, "All I know is he was in the military and was hurt in some kind of attack. While he was being treated, he met the nurse."

Jean-Philippe stared at her. "I don't believe it."

"What is it?" she asked, alarmed by his expression. "What's wrong?"

"Do you know where—what part of his body—suffered the wound?"

"He was shot in the leg, but worse was some kind of damage to his lungs. Why?"

Jean-Philippe's face paled at her words and then he asked, "What's his name?"

"All I know is Luke."

"*Luke?*" The word was a harsh whisper.

She stared at him. "What's going on? Why do you care about my neighbor?"

He shut his eyes, but when he opened them again, he looked up at Elijah's portrait. "Luke ... Lucas. Like the son, the ghost."

She couldn't believe the way he was acting. "So what? You

can*not* be implying ... A lot of guys are named Luke, or Lucas! It's a very popular name in this area."

He kept looking from the sketch to the portrait. "You said that Lucas Donnelly, the son, painted the portrait of Elijah, correct?"

"That's what I was told."

"Look." He handed her the sketch book, pointing from it to Elijah's portrait. The confusion in his expression combined with what she saw caused her nerves to stand on end. She was enough of an artist to recognize a definite similarity in the style of the sketch to that of the painting. "Can you explain what you're seeing?" he asked.

No, she thought, I can't. Her mouth went dry. There had to be an explanation. But what? "I see what you mean," she began, wracking her brain. "It's a definite style. Maybe ... maybe an art teacher lives in the area and studied the 'primitive' style of Lucas Donnelly and passed it on to ...to others. And maybe one of them was my neighbor, Luke."

At his dismissive frown at her theory, she tried to think of something plausible, and finally came up with an idea. "Are you, perhaps, thinking my neighbor is an offspring of the first Lucas Donnelly? I doubt it because that would make him part of my family. Someone in town would have mentioned it. You can't keep secrets like that in a small town."

Jean-Philippe's brow furrowed as he continued to study Elijah's portrait. "Frankly, I don't know what to think. Does your neighbor also do portraits in oil?"

"He said he once did." She eyed him. "Tell me why this is so important to you."

"Where does he live?"

She rubbed her forehead, troubled by his questions, by how bothered he was by all this. It made no sense. "All I know is he's a neighbor."

"Which house?"

"I don't know! He walks to the river and I've seen him take the dirt road past the cabin. He said his house isn't very close."

"I want to meet him."

She eyed him, her gaze hard. "Why? Jean-Philippe, what's this about?"

"All right. It's probably only fair that I show you." He took out his wallet. From it he slid out a small, very old photograph, one with a thick white border and scalloped edges, the sort of photograph created back when they were considered something rare and lovely. He handed it to her. "This is my great-grandmother, Claire Dupont. She was a nurse in France during *La Grande Guerre*, or what you Americans call World War I."

Julia studied the photo and then looked at the sketch. Luke was an excellent sketch artist and his drawing was quite realistic. "I don't understand. Why does your great-grandmother look so much like the sketch that Luke drew?"

"That's the question, isn't it?"

She shook her head. "They must be relatives. Luke didn't tell me anything about who his nurse was, what nationality, or even what country he was in when he met her. I assumed he was in the U.S., but he might have been in Europe."

He rubbed his hand over his mouth. "Perhaps," he whispered finally.

She looked again at the photograph and then at him. Something wasn't right. "Frankly, I've never heard of anyone carrying their great-grandmother's photo around. So why are you doing it?" When he didn't answer right away, her irritation grew. "What do you know that you're not telling me? There is clearly something else going on here!"

He walked to the French doors and looked out onto the back porch. The morning dew was icy, and the porch glistened. Then, he turned to face her. "All I can say is, when I learned about the cabin and its ghosts—from the newspaper exposé about it, by the way—I thought I needed to come here and to bring the photo with me. I was expecting to find someone who might have heard about her. It seems I was right." He faced her, his expression sterner and harsher than she'd ever seen it. "There are many possible reasons why two women who lived a hundred years apart have such similar features. I'm here for the answer."

"But what led you from the article about the cabin and its ghosts to your great-grandmother and Luke's nurse? It makes no sense."

"It does to me." He stopped talking, his jaw firm. He said nothing more as he walked to the door.

"Wait, Jean-Philippe!" she called. But he didn't stop and left the cabin.

CHAPTER 13

When Jean-Philippe returned to the cabin that evening, he saw Julia sitting on the sofa by the fire, her face aglow in its light. Her laptop was open, and he guessed she'd been working on some design. She hadn't talked about doing them, but he'd passed by her working often enough that he'd picked up on the kind of work she did. Probably because she needed the money.

Now, however, her blue-green eyes were filled with curiosity as she looked up at him.

He had to admit, as he'd become accustomed to her different look—the almost white hair, the dark brows and long-lashes, small nose, full lips, and oddly colored eyes that met his with such frankness he was sometimes startled—he found her increasingly lovely with each passing day.

He did his best to shake off the feeling, knowing that after she learned his story, she might decide he was mad and demand that he leave. He wouldn't blame her. But he wasn't about to go anywhere until he found the answers he'd come here for.

And once he did, he'd be glad to shake the strangeness of this place from his heels.

From the moment he walked into the cabin, he could feel something here. He'd never experienced anything like it. A presence? More than one? He had no idea. He knew he shouldn't believe in such things. No sane, twenty-first century fellow his age would believe such rubbish. But Grandmere had believed in them, and she was the wisest person he'd ever met. And as she grew older, she became ever more convinced that the veil between this world and the next was quite thin.

He took a deep breath. The strange things he'd witnessed here with Julia, and all he'd learned about her neighbor, Lucas, pointed him in a direction Grandmere would have understood.

He should be frightened of what he was seeing and feeling, like the CD player, or the mouse that chased Crystal around the room. Julia had excuses for them, but CD players didn't work the way she was saying, and Crystal wouldn't have the imagination to decide a dead mouth was chasing her anywhere. No, something was in effect here, and why he didn't pack his bags and run from it was probably a good indication of his own degree of madness.

"How are you?" Julia asked. "You're looking at me strangely."

He shook away his wayward thoughts. "I'm sorry. It's just that I've puzzled all day about the drawing that looks so much like my great-grandmother. And I've thought about how to tell you everything I know, wondering what your reaction will be."

She stood. "You're making me nervous, Jean-Philippe. I don't like this one bit."

"It's all right, nothing to be afraid of," he murmured. "Sit please. It's upstairs. I'll get it."

A brief moment later, he approached Julia holding a leather-covered journal, its pages held together with a thin leather strap. "I probably should have told you about this much earlier, but I think you'll understand why I hesitated to when you see it." He handed her the journal. "It belonged to my great-grand-mother, Claire Dumont."

Julia's lips were tight, her eyes determined as she took the journal and untied the strap. The entries were written with a fountain pen using a small, delicate penmanship—and it was in French. The pages had yellowed somewhat, and the ink had faded to light brown. She tried to read it, but soon handed it back. "My high school French won't help me with this, I'm afraid."

"I'm not surprised," he said. "Much of it is almost in a kind of shorthand of day-to-day notes and events, people, comings and goings. But some is much more detailed, and much more important. Most of it was written during World War One."

"Can you translate for me?"

"Of course. But before I do, you need to know that when France and Germany went to war in 1914, many men joined the battle immediately. We lost over two million men in that war. The U.S. entered it much later. But for France, it started early and was horrible. Claire married in 1914, and her young husband, Raymond Dumont, was one of the first sent off to fight."

"She must have been terrified for him," Julia said.

"Very. It's all here in her diary. He was only twenty-two, and she was twenty-one at the time. But then, in 1915, his letters stopped. Many men were dying on the battlefield, and the dead were not always identified. She knew that. His family accepted what had happened to him, but Claire held out hope that he had been injured. She went to many hospitals searching for him among the wounded and dying. She couldn't find him, but what she saw changed her.

"She volunteered to help wounded soldiers in hospitals. Since so much of the fighting took place in or close to France, the wounded from many countries ended up in French hospitals. In 1917, since the Americans had also joined the war effort, we began to see your soldiers in our hospitals. One of those soldiers was named Lucas Donnelly. I wasn't sure when I came here, but now I'm positive that soldier was the cabin's Lucas Donnelly."

Julia made no comment but he could tell she was listening with rapt attention.

He leafed through the book. He'd read it more than once and quickly found what he was looking for. "Here is her first mention of him."

He translated as he read:

A young American, Lucas Donnelly, was placed in my ward. He was badly wounded in the leg, but as long as I can keep it clean of infection, it will not be a problem. But his lungs sound very bad. I tried to find a doctor to check on him, but they are too busy trying to keep men from dying. Lucas looks at me with such fear, but also hope, I told him I will do all I can to keep him alive. He doesn't understand a word I say, but he seems to understand the meaning behind the words.

"His injuries," Julia whispered, then met his gaze, her face incredulous.

"Yes, they were the same as your neighbor's."

Her chin rose. "Coincidence, that's all."

"Of course," Jean-Philippe murmured.

"It could be," Julia said, growing irritated by questions he knew she couldn't answer—that no one could answer. "Go on," she insisted.

"Claire talks about other patients as well, and some that she couldn't help," he explained as he turned the pages. "The journal is heartbreaking to read. But, as the days go by, it soon becomes clear that her visits with Lucas became the highlight of her day. She taught him some French, he taught her some English, and somehow they were able to communicate completely. He was her success story. But he continued to suffer from what she thought was pneumonia. His breathing became more and more labored and although the leg wound was healing nicely, he couldn't leave the hospital. She checked on him every day, and when he didn't grow stronger, she knew there was still something wrong."

"So was he was gassed during the war?" Julia asked. "Like my neighbor was?"

"Actually, by the time the Americans entered, many of them were given gas masks, so gas warfare wasn't as effective as it had been in the early years. But the troops fought a sickness as lethal, although slower, than the gasses used. When Claire finally was able to get a doctor to take the time to check on Lucas, the doctor found he had tuberculosis."

Julia placed her fingertips to her lips. "And at that time, there was no cure for it, was there?"

"No." His voice was hushed. "It was a death sentence. It could be held off for a while by getting a lot of rest and fresh air to breathe, in other words, making the lungs work as little as possible. It was the leading cause of death in most of the world, including the United States, during that time. The living conditions in the army during the war, the cold, the damp, living in close quarters that couldn't be cleaned well, the exhaustion from combat and lack of sleep, poor food, and so on, led to many men becoming infected with it.

"As soon as the authorities learned Lucas had tuberculosis, he was sent to a special ward for TB patients, away from the others. Claire realized that Lucas had been sent there to die. The doctors, short-handed due to the war, knew the disease was incurable and so spent their valuable time helping those who had a chance to survive.

"But Claire was determined to save Lucas. By this time, the two were desperately in love. Claire worked hard, even badgering American officers to give him a medical discharge from the Army, and once that went through, she moved him into her little home in the village. He applied to be allowed to stay in France. The government was barely able to function during this time, and no one paid much attention to the sick American. Claire wrote about their time together." He turned to a page. "I wish you understood the French because it doesn't sound nearly as beautiful in my poor English, but I will try my best to tell you what she wrote:

I will not leave my Lucas to die alone. God has sent him to me to heal my empty heart even though I know, unless a miracle happens, we won't have many years together. That is not our future. But such a future means nothing to me. I have seen too much death and waste. I went to him last night and held him close despite his fears for my health. He pleaded with me to leave his bed, but I refused. I told him we must love now, capture the moment that is given us. When God takes him from me to end his suffering, to end the devastation befalling his beautiful body, I can only hope I will soon follow because without him, my life has no meaning. In his arms, I have never known such joy or such sorrow. He is everything to me.

"Dear God," Julia whispered. "It sounds as if she no longer cared about herself. That they'd both given up."

Jean-Philippe's heart was always heavy when he came to that part of Claire's journal. "They had given in to despair. Also, Lucas was having trouble getting permission to stay in France. What little government France had, didn't want to admit an American dying of tuberculosis. They kept putting off approving his application to remain in the country. But then, the two lovers were given some news."

Julia waited as he turned a couple of pages and translated them for her.

I could not believe what has happened, so I went to my doctor to be sure. I am with child, and my lungs, thanks be to God, remain free of the dreaded disease. Lucas says we must take care to protect our child and to protect me, although it hurts me not to hold him and love him as I once did. He believes that, although I have been strong enough to fight off this illness, when carrying a child, I might be in a weakened state and might catch the illness from him. We cried tears of both joy and sadness at this strange turn of events. But I see this baby as hope for us both. Hope that, somehow, Lucas will get better and will see his child grow strong and healthy. I won't allow him to die. I won't! He and our child are the joys of my life. I have never felt so blessed or so happy.

Julia shook her head. "It's hard to listen to her happiness, knowing that, for some reason, Lucas came back here alone to die. Was it the French government that wouldn't let him stay?"

Jean-Philippe drew in his breath. "No. The reason was much more difficult. Here, let me read you a bit more:

I was making barley soup for Lucas for his lunch when I heard a church bell begin to chime. I thought I was hearing things, because the bells had been silenced during the war. But then I heard another, and another.

I ran out to the street and watched it fill with people cheering and shouting, "The war is over." News wires transmitted that on the eleventh day of the eleventh month at eleven o'clock in the morning, Germany signed an armistice, an agreement for peace. After so very much death and heartache, the war had finally ended, and church bells throughout the city, throughout the entire country, rang out the good news. I ran inside and told Lucas. We held each other and gave prayers of thanks. Life truly is good.

And we decided, in that moment, that if the French government will not allow Lucas to stay in France, that I and our child will go with him to America. There, we shall begin a new life, and somehow, Lucas will survive. He must!

Julia's heart sank. "Tell me that their happiness lasted for quite a while."

"No, only three days," he said. And as he read Claire's powerful words, Julia could picture it, as if she were there...

***

Lucas and Claire were having lunch in Claire's little house and talking about their future—a future they scarcely dared to dream they might have—when they heard a knock on the door.

Claire answered it to find Raymond's parents standing before her. They were old and short, and huddled together as if needing to hold each other up. The years of war, deprivation, and loss had ravaged their faces and bodies, and left them looking even older than they were.

Claire stood stiffly facing them. "Please come in." She was a tall woman with brown hair so dark it was nearly black and she wore it loosely pulled back and pinned up. Her eyes were brown, and her lashes long and dark.

When she first brought Lucas to the house that she and Raymond had shared as husband and wife, his parents had refused to speak to her. But after a while, their hearts softened. They understood about Lucas's illness, and when they learned Claire was expecting a child, they gave her their blessing, recognizing that life must go on, even if without Raymond. Claire was grateful that they had accepted her attempt to find happiness again, although relations between them would be forever strained.

Now, the look on their faces frightened her. "What's wrong?" she asked.

Raymond's mother, Simone, burst into tears. "He's alive."

Claire said nothing. Her mind seemed to go numb, and Simone's words could not, would not, make sense.

"Raymond is alive." Simone all but shouted. Then she put both gnarled hands to her lips a moment as she gathered the strength to explain. "He was captured and held prisoner all these years. An officer came to visit us this afternoon, to give us the news. He said he first came to see you—Raymond's wife. But then he saw you and Lucas together, and saw your condition. He's a good man, a sensitive man, and so he sought us out instead."

Claire just stared at Simone and Georges, Raymond's father. Georges kept his head high, his back rigid, and offered no understanding, no compassion. Claire folded her arms over the child she carried and bowed her head. "I do thank God he's alive, I do. How is he? Where is he?"

Simone continued. "The officer said Raymond is in a hospital—malnourished, skin and bones, sores on his flesh from the way he was treated—but with care, in time, he should grow strong. They will send him home in two days. He can stay at our house, but he is still your husband, Claire. Your husband!"

Claire couldn't move and had no idea what to do. The world began to spin faster and faster. Raymond had been the love of her life, and she felt as if she had died when she thought he had been killed. But now she had Lucas and their child.

Simone and Georges looked at Lucas, then turned and walked out the door without another word.

"Claire," Lucas whispered. He put his arms around her and walked her toward a chair.

"Luke! My God, Luke, what are we going to do?" She clutched him as tears streamed down her face.

He helped her to sit and then knelt at her side, his arms around her as he rested his head against her stomach to listen to his child's heartbeat. Her arms circled his head and shoulders, all but crushing him to her. They stayed that way a long time.

He wiped his tears before he looked at her again. "I must leave."

"No!" Her hands caressed his face, brushing back his dark

brown hair, as her gaze met gray eyes that looked at her with such love. "Please, you can't."

"He's your husband. I know how much you loved him and now he's alive. You heard his parents. He suffered in the German prison, and I can't help but suspect thoughts of you were what kept him going—just as you made me want to live. You kept me alive, Claire. But now, it's time for me to step aside. I know I'm dying. I know I don't have long to care for you and our child."

She sobbed. "No, you can't go, Luke. I won't let you. I love you!"

"I know you do." He stood, then bent and kissed her forehead. "And I love you more than life itself. I'll always be with you—in your heart, with our child. I only hope your husband will accept the little one. If he doesn't, perhaps your mother or your sister will, or you'll be able to find a good family…"

"No! I'll never let our child go. Never. That I promise you."

She stood and paced back and forth across the room. "We'll leave France right away," she said. "We'll do it!"

She spun toward Lucas now, her grief and desperation frightening. "May God help me. I prayed for his return so many times, and I am thankful he's alive. But I can't let you leave me, Luke! I can't bear it. Please, I beg you!"

"You make sure he gets well, Claire. You can do it. I'm a lost cause, but he isn't."

"No, you aren't! You're getting stronger. I can see it every day. Every day!"

"Until the next relapse," he murmured.

"Please stay with me." Her tears came so hard she could scarcely speak.

He couldn't argue with her any longer. "I'll always be with you," he repeated.

"Promise me," she demanded.

"Yes."

It took some time before she was able to relax enough to fall asleep that night, but once she did, he arose, glanced at the painting he had started—it would have been of Claire if he'd had time to finish it—and quietly packed his few belongings. Last of all, he wrote her a note.

My dearest Claire,

Life has been good. It brought you to me. With you, for the first time in my life, I learned what it means to truly love, to have joy, and to know happiness. You are everything to me.

I remember when we first met, and you told me about your husband, and how everyone told you he had been killed even though there was no official "proof." You swore that, in your heart, you knew he was alive. You told me how much you loved him. I envied him—a dead man—that love. And only slowly did you come to accept his death, and even more slowly, did you allow your heart to open to mine.

Now, it turns out that you were right all along. He is alive.

And as much as I wish it weren't so, I am dying.

I will pray every day until my last breath that the love you had for him returns stronger than ever in your heart, and that all he felt for you will bring him understanding and forgiveness of the situation in which you now find yourself. And that he will accept our child and be a good father to our little one.

May you be happy again, my beautiful Claire. Know I will love you and our child forever and, if it be possible, beyond life and time itself.

Luke

"I can't imagine such heartbreak," Julia whispered as she blinked back her tears.

Jean-Philippe nodded. "Claire and Lucas had a daughter. Claire named her Adele. Adele was my grandmother—Grandmere. After Lucas left, Claire wrote nothing more in her journal. Grandmere told me what little she knew about what happened afterward."

Julia waited in silence for Jean-Philippe to conclude his story. "Grandmere learned that Raymond, Claire's husband, was very sick when he returned. He slowly recovered, but apparently the years in prison had changed him and he was no longer the loving, jovial man Claire had fallen in love with. But he accepted Claire's child, Adele, into his home. Grandmere once told me she felt Raymond had never completely forgiven Claire for her affair with Lucas Donnelly. But Raymond had been a kind father to her.

"Claire and Raymond never had any children—perhaps a sign of the state of their marriage. Also, Grandmere grew up knowing that Raymond wasn't her biological father. When she was young, she had been told that her mother had thought she was a widow and had actually married her American father, but then divorced him and went back to Raymond after it was learned he was alive. But there were too many people around for Adele not to have heard rumors that there was a lot more to the story of her mother and the American soldier than she'd been told. Sometimes, Grandmere told me, when kids got mad at her about something, they'd call her the illegitimate brat of an American soldier who had deserted her and her mother, only the words they'd used were a lot harsher than 'illegitimate brat.'"

"Children can be very cruel at times," Julia said with a shake of the head.

"True. But it wasn't until after Claire's death that Adele

found this journal and Lucas's last letter to Claire, and learned the truth."

"I see," Julia said, and then added, "Did you notice that Claire called him Luke?"

"I did." He nodded, then drew in his breath. "Grandmere, Adele, like so many French women of her generation, married a soldier and lost him during the Second World War. Their only child was my mother. Claire suggested a name for the baby, Lucienne. Adele didn't learn until she read the journal why Claire had suggested the female version of the name Lucas."

"Claire still loved him," Julia murmured.

"She did. And I know that's a good part of the reason Grandmere always wondered about her real father and what had happened to him after he left France. She knew that her mother had always hoped he had somehow managed to live many years despite his illness.

"I also suspected one reason Grandmere spent so much time with me in the United States, particularly when I was young and attending boarding schools in New York, was that she was quietly searching, trying to find out what had happened to him. But we had only the faintest idea as to what part of the U.S. he was from. Claire had told Grandmere only that her father was from a wild part of the country that she had never heard of, a place where men wore cowboy hats and boots and rode horses. She found it all quite exciting. But Grandmere and I soon learn the American West was huge and had many Lucas Donnellys, and very poor records, including those from World War One."

"Makes sense," Julia said. "And I can understand Adele wanting to know more about her real father. I'm glad Claire wanted her granddaughter named after Lucas. I think it shows the depth of her love for him even though circumstances caused her to remain with her first—her only—husband."

The temperature in the room suddenly dropped, and Julia shivered. "The fire has gone out. It's freezing in here."

"It is," Jean-Philippe agreed. They added logs and stood together by the hearth as he continued. "In any case, Grandmere always found her parents' story very sad, but intriguing. Even when she was dying, she said she hoped I would not give up my search for Lucas. And that, if it is possible when she was on 'the other side,' as she called it, once I learned what had happened to him, she would know as well. It's a lovely thought—and I hope it's so."

"And if it is true," Julia said, her eyes widening, "that means you are Lucas Donnelly's great-grandson. His heir."

Her speaking of inheritance made him realize where her thoughts might be turning. "If you're worried about the cabin, somehow, it went from Lucas to your part of the family. Didn't you say Lucas gave it to his cousin?"

"Yes, my great-grandfather, Theodore."

"So, it turns out that my great-grandfather, Lucas, and yours, Theodore, were cousins. That means we, too, are cousins," he said.

She nodded. "Distant cousins many, many times removed, whatever that means. But if Lucas didn't know he had a child when he gave away the cabin …"

"Julia, please. I'm not here to take your cabin. I'm here to learn about my family, to fulfill the wish my grandmother told me when she died. I don't know if there will be more evidence, but I only wish she had lived to see this place. I think she would have liked it here."

Julia's eyes searched his face, as if trying to decide whether she could believe him. He guessed, finally, she did because she said, "It seems your grandmother had a very fine, long life."

"She did. Ninety-nine years," he added. "May we all be so fortunate."

"And she had you." Still facing the fire, she touched his arm. "It is nice the two of you were so close. Good for both of you, I think."

"I miss her every day," he said. "Especially now, here, with you and all this. There's so much I wish I could tell her."

"If your great-grandfather and the cabin's Lucas Donnelly are one and the same person, I'm glad to know his story. He was always a mystery to us."

Jean-Philippe nodded. "I can imagine why he didn't tell many people what had happened to him. And I can understand why he would have come here to be alone and to wait what he knew would be inevitable."

"That poor man," Julia whispered.

Her compassion warmed him and he took her hand. "But, at least he knew what it meant to know love. And, he had a wonderful daughter who had a rich, complete life, and was well loved and appreciated by her family."

She let him go and stepped aside.

His eyes dropped, and he nodded, looking suddenly sad and lonely. "You're right, the hour is late. Goodnight, Julia. Thank you for listening."

He turned away.

"Wait." She put her arms around him in a quick hug. "Thank you for telling me. Goodnight, now."

The surprising warmth of her touch surrounded him, capturing his breath. He, too, whispered, "Goodnight," and then quietly went upstairs.

CHAPTER 14

Julia was surprised when Jean-Philippe didn't go to the forest early the next morning the way he usually did. Instead he told her that he wanted to go with her to the river at the time she usually met her neighbor, Luke. She agreed to let him know before she left the house.

She didn't quite know what to say to him after all the revelations of the night before, and he, too, seemed awkward and uneasy. She couldn't quite bring herself to greet him with a "Hiya, cuz!" And thank goodness, he didn't try that with her.

Finally, he took his coffee up to his room, saying he needed to do some reading.

When the time came, Julia led him to the riverbank. She was glad she took her paints and set up her easel because Jean-Philippe wasn't at all talkative. All he did was pace.

After an hour, she felt Luke wasn't going to show up, but Jean-Philippe insisted on waiting another half-hour. As soon as the time was up, she gathered her paint supplies. "We should go back to the cabin."

"Maybe he's jealous of the time the two of you spend together," Jean-Philippe eyed her. "Maybe he doesn't want a stranger interrupting his time with you."

"No," she said firmly. "It's not that kind of relationship, although I do suspect he doesn't have many friends."

"You mean he has no feelings for you?"

"I think he cares about me, but not the way you mean.," she said. "From the way he talked about his nurse, I think he still loves her. Only her. Anyway, we can try again tomorrow."

"What about you?" he asked, his tone low and somewhat morose as they started up the hill to the cabin. "You speak so gently about him. I think you love him."

She gawked at him. "I don't 'love' him. But I'll admit that I care about him more than makes sense considering how little I know him. Something about him, from the time we first met, drew me close. It's like a bond, but a purely platonic bond. I can't explain it, and I have no idea why, but I won't deny it's there."

His brows crossed. "You're sure that's all it is?"

"Yes, I'm sure." Her large blue-green eyes captured his, and she gave a hint of a smile. If she didn't know better, she'd say he sounded jealous. But obviously, that wasn't the case.

He reached over and took the portable easel from her without a word and carried it the rest of the way to the cabin.

When they reached the cabin, he said, "I need to leave, to check on some things in the Boise forest."

"Oh, my God! With the talk about the sketch, I forgot to tell you. Yesterday while I was with Luke at the river, we saw what may have been a gyrfalcon! It was mostly white with some gray —a beautiful bird."

His eyes widened "Really? About how big was it?"

She thought a moment. "It was about the size of a rooster, I'd say.

"Let me show you pictures of gyrs to make sure it was what

you saw," he said excitedly. "If it seemed that large, it was probably a female. They're actually about double most male gyrs."

He called up some images on his phone to show her.

"That looks exactly like what I saw, and Luke called them 'arctic falcons.' He sounded pretty sure."

"Yes!" Jean-Philippe's hands clenched, and he raised them to the sky. "She made it past the smugglers! Good for her! Ah, *cherie!*" He grabbed her and spun her around. "This is great news."

She wrapped her arms around his shoulders, enjoying his happiness. When he put her down, she kept her arms around him. "I want to go with you today. Into the forest."

"Really?" At her nod, they let each other go. "Okay, I'll pack some food while you dress warm. It's freezing out there!"

Julia sat quietly, taking in the desolate area as Jean-Philippe drove his truck over an increasingly narrow and bumpy dirt road into the Boise National Forest. The road followed the river, but steep mountains rose high above it on both sides of the waterway.

Jean-Philippe stopped at a small forest ranger outpost and parked.

"There are three biologists like me working with the U.S. Fish and Wildlife Service and Idaho's Fish and Game," Jean-Philippe said as he took out a key and unlocked a shed at a ranger outpost. Inside was an ATV. He moved their backpacks —his with a first aid kit, logbook, and birding equipment, and Julia's with food and water—from the truck into the ATV. "We form a local team, but Fish and Wildlife has been running an undercover operation in other parts of the country for nearly two years trying to get as much information as possible to round up the entire smuggling operation. Those reports show this is where they've captured the most gyrfalcons, and a high number of peregrines."

Julia was surprised to learn the federal agencies were involved. "How long has the local operation been going on?"

"This phase started a couple of weeks before I got here. But we can't keep it going very long. The smugglers will spot us soon, if they haven't already."

"So, the smugglers live out here?" she asked, eying the stark, barren area beyond one of the few roads in the forest.

"Or close by. They need to put live bait—rodents, small birds, and such—into their traps to lure the falcons."

Julia understood what he was saying. "So since Crouch is the closest town, they might go to it for their own food and supplies. And that means someone there might know them."

"Yes, but I thought Crouch gets a lot of hunters, fishermen, and tourists passing through," he said.

"The colder and snowier it gets, the fewer strangers will be there. And the residents tend to recognize each other. If there's anything odd about the smugglers, townspeople will spot it. In fact, I know a few people I can ask."

"That could help us. So, are you ready?"

The ATV was a two-seater. They rode for over a half-hour before Jean-Philippe stopped. He shoved the ATV under some brush to hide it.

After inputting the location to his team, Jean-Philippe took the lead on an uphill hike and helped Julia whenever they reached a steep or difficult spot.

Finally, they reached the top of the ridge. Julia loved the sight of the valley carved by the Middle Fork of the Payette River far below them, open and wild. She noticed how Jean-Philippe's eyes carefully followed the slope of the mountains down to the river, then up and outward. He then dropped down into the brush and set up his spotting scope. Out in this wilderness she saw a completely new side of the man. Here, he was in his element, a serious, knowledgeable scientist on a mission to protect innocent creatures. She liked and admired what she was seeing.

She took the binoculars Jean-Philippe provided her, and the two sat scouring the terrain for any sign of disturbance or human involvement. They watched for a couple of hours with no success. Finally, Jean-Philippe suggested they have some lunch before moving to a different location.

As they ate, Julia brought up a question she'd had for some time. "You never mention your family except for your grandmother. Are your parents still living? Any brothers or sisters?"

"My parents are quite healthy," he began. "My mother is a violinist, mostly retired now and living in the south of France. For years she was second chair with the Berlin Philharmonic and she also belonged to a string quartet that performed when Berlin's season was over."

"I've heard Berlin has one of the best orchestras in the world," Julia said, impressed. "She must be outstanding."

"She is. Music is everything to her. My father is a judge. He'll never retire. The two married late in life and soon after I was born, they divorced."

"I'm sorry," Julia said.

"No need. I don't even remember us together as a family. My mother traveled a lot with the orchestra and her string quartet, while my father hated being away from his work. I think both my parents were more interested in their careers than in their child, which was why my grandmother took over raising me."

"I suspect she was glad to take care of you," Julia said.

"I think so. Grandmere never let anything hold her back if at all possible. You remember me talking about her mother's house, the one Claire brought Lucas Donnelly to live in with her. Well, after Claire and Raymond Dumont died, it became Grandmere's home. She sold it and used the money to help buy a small house in Paris. She rented out the rooms to boarders." He looked at Julia and smiled. "Sound familiar? Anyway, when she got a little money ahead, she used it to buy another house and rented out its rooms. She kept doing that and before she knew it, she was buying apartment buildings. Also, one of her boarders knew a young fashion designer whose name was Hubert de Givenchy. Grandmere liked his style and invested in him as he set out to launch his first collection of dresses in the 1950s. She had an instinct for good investments, and Givenchy was the first of many. Because of that, she could pay for violin lessons for my mother, for my education, and for us to travel the world together."

"She sounds amazing," Julia said. "And since you inherited from her, that must mean you can afford to stay anywhere in the world, yet you're staying in my little cabin because of Lucas Donnelly?"

"And because I like it there," he said.

Something about the way he said that warmed her. "Well, I'm glad to hear it. And, I guess when you can afford to do whatever you'd like, using your time to try to save birds from a terrible existence at the hands of smugglers is a good thing."

He looked pleased. "I like that you think so, Julia."

Her gaze searched his face, the openness, the truth with which he spoke to her. She'd never met a man like him before. It was a bewildering feeling. "I do," she said frankly.

When Jean-Philippe had finished his sandwich, he returned to his scope, sitting on the ground and moving it slightly toward the right to take one last survey of the area before he packed up. "Don't tell me," he muttered after a while.

"What is it?"

"A bal-chatri. It's one of the more common traps for falcons. Come here and look."

He put his arm around her to steady her as she knelt to look through the scope. "You can see a wire cage. It's got a bunch of clear filament nooses all over it. Inside is a bait animal. When the falcon lands on the cage trying to grab the animal that lured it, the bird's talons get ensnared in the nooses and it's stuck there until the smuggler comes along, takes hold of it and untangles its feet."

"Oh, yuck! A live mouse is in the trap now," Julia said, moving back with a shudder. "So the smugglers must be around here somewhere."

"Definitely. I'll report the finding, but I'm getting you out of here. If we can see the trap from here, if the smugglers are nearby, they'll be able to see us as well." Jean-Philippe took out his satellite phone and began punching in numbers to send the trap's coordinates to the base.

Julia stood, staring out at the skies. "Oh, no. Jean-Philippe, look!" She gripped his shoulder. "Is it a falcon?"

"What?" He looked up to see where she was pointing and gasped. "No, no!" He stood and started to wave his arms, hoping to divert the large bird, but it did no good.

"It's caught," he said. "I've got to free it."

"But what if the smugglers are near? And they might have already seen you, waving and shouting."

"That wasn't smart, was it?" He thought a moment. "I suspect if they were near, they'd already be out there grabbing the bird. It looks like a peregrine—worth several thousand dollars on the black market. We'll get as close as possible, and if we don't see them—or them us—we'll free that bird, then run to the ATV and get out of here."

"Got it," she said.

They quickly gathered their belongings and Jean-Philippe

held her hand as he hurried down the mountainside to the bird, knowing the sooner he got to it, the less it might hurt itself in its struggle to break free of the filament that its long, curved talons were caught in.

Julia was appalled at how hard the bird was flapping its wings and trying to escape, sometimes lifting the entire trap in the air, only to fall back hard to earth. The mouse inside was running in frantic circles.

They crouched behind a thick fir that provided cover even as winter approached. "The fastest way to free the peregrine," Jean-Philippe said, "will be for you to cut the filament while I hold the bird. Just be careful not to let its talons gouge you."

Julia nervously nodded. Jean-Philippe handed her small, sharp-pointed scissors from his backpack, then put on thick gloves and grabbed a cloth. "Ready?"

She wondered about her own gloves, but then realized it would be impossible to use the scissors wearing them. The closer she got to the bird, the more sharp and deadly its beak and talons appeared. And it's weird, staring eyes were especially unnerving. Jean-Philippe put a cloth over its head, carefully wrapped his arm around the wings so they wouldn't flap and then lifted the bird. It seemed to go limp, but its talons were curled tight as Julia struggled to cut the filament cords and then untangle them and pull them free. The filament was harder to cut than she'd expected, but the scissors were quite sharp.

She was half-way finished when they heard a gunshot.

They both froze.

"It's a rifle," Jean-Philippe said. "Hurry!"

They heard another shot, and Julia didn't care how much it hurt her fingers, she bore down hard on those filament cords cutting them as quickly as she could while Jean-Philippe held the terrified bird. "Done, I think," she said.

Jean-Philippe made sure the bird's feet were free, set it on the ground, and removed the cloth. Two more shots were quickly fired. Julia ran toward the shelter of the fir trees, but Jean-Philippe wasn't with her. She stopped and looked back. She saw the falcon flap its wings and take off, free, as Jean-Philippe raced back to the bal-chatri. He opened the trap and tipped it so the mouse could also escape. Then, still holding the trap, he ran to where Julia watched.

He scarcely hesitated, but grabbed her hand and headed down the mountain. When they reached another thick stand of firs, he dived into it, and then stopped so they could catch their breaths.

"What were those shots?" she asked, winded.

He looked worried. "Four shots. It probably means they found the ATV, shot out its tires."

"Oh, God!" She leaned against the tree truck, then bent forward, her hand against her thighs, still breathing heavily. "What are we going to do?"

"Don't worry. Most likely, they think it belongs to people on a hike and they're leaving a message to stay away from this area."

She didn't believe that for a minute, but knew he was trying to calm her fears. "And, if that's not the case?" she couldn't help but ask.

"If not, they know they've been found and they'll want to stop us from leaving."

He took her hand and crouching low, ran to another stand of trees, then both knelt down in the brush and scoured the area. "I'm really sorry, Julia. This has never been dangerous before. It's been dull, to tell the truth."

"No need to apologize. With smugglers involved, I knew the chance of danger existed. But they should know that to hurt us would cause them a lot more grief than smuggling. We'll be okay."

"Unless they're really desperate," Jean-Philippe added, his face etched with the peril they might face.

"I can't imagine—"

"Listen to me." His eyes bore into hers, all pretext of this being 'nothing' gone now. "For the most part, the people doing this are bottom feeders who don't care what damage they do to wildlife. All they want is money. And they'll do anything to stop whoever is in their way. Anything. Am I clear?"

She nodded. "Very."

"Let's move while we have daylight," Jean-Philippe said, gripping her hand. "We need to go as fast as possible and hope we can reach the truck before they do. They might realize they can simply follow the tracks from the ATV to find it."

They started scurrying down the mountain but as they crossed a treeless expanse, they heard a shot and saw a cloud of smoke nearby as a shot pinged off some rocky soil. The smugglers had found them and were shooting at them.

"Run!" Jean-Philippe shouted, pulling Julia toward some pines. Julia somehow managed to remain on her feet, knowing that if she fell one or both of them could end up dead.

They reached the trees as several more shots sailed close by.

"We've got to get to the truck," Jean-Philippe said. "We'll zigzag as much as possible and try to lose them. Can you do it?"

"I can," she said, thankful she often went hiking. Running was different ... but every so often, the ping of a bullet striking nearby was quite the incentive to keep going and to move fast.

They found a hollow in the hillside where they could stop a moment to catch their breaths. "Well, the good news is they're following us rather than the ATV's tracks," Jean-Philippe said.

"That's good news?" Julia wasn't buying it.

"Hopefully."

Jean-Philippe and Julia stuck to the trees as they ran. They caught glimpses more than once of the two people hunting them. They appeared to be two men—one larger and one smaller—but between heavy parkas and caps with earflaps their features and even hair colors were hidden.

"They're still dogging us," Jean-Philippe said. "I think we should circle away from the truck, then head back up the mountain. That might confuse them into thinking they've lost us. You up for it?"

"I'd better be," Julia said with a nod.

"That's the spirit."

He led the way, and Julia made sure she kept up with him. After a while, they no longer saw the two who had been following them, and heard no more gunshots. The sun was already low on the horizon, since sunset came early in the Idaho mountains in winter. Carefully, they made their way down to the truck.

When they reached the ranger outpost where they'd left the truck, fog and mist had rolled in off the river, blanketing the moon and stars and making the night practically pitch black. "Wait here while I get the truck," Jean-Philippe said. "Be ready to jump in when I pull up."

She grabbed his arm. "What if they've found it already?"

"There's no other way. We need it to get away from here."

She all but stop breathing. "No, you can't—"

"I've got to."

She knew the truth of his words. Then she nodded.

In two steps, she could no longer see him. She only hoped he knew where he was going and how to get out of here. She waited. All remained quiet.

But then, she heard the truck's engine rev. And she began to breathe again. The backup lights were the only ones on as Jean-Philippe careened backward to where Julia waited. He pushed open the passenger door. Heart pounding, she ran to the truck and jumped in.

To find their way out of the area, to simply find the dirt road, he had no choice but to turn on the headlights. Sure enough, as he peeled away, they heard shots. But the smugglers must have been some distance away because nothing hit the truck.

"We made it!" Julia cried as they reached the cabin. She ran to the front door opened, it, petted the cats who greeted her, and as soon as Jean-Philippe entered, she locked the door behind him and threw her arms around him. "You did it! And I've never been so happy to get back home! You save my life! Both our lives!"

"After I endangered them, you mean. Again, I never meant to put you in harm's way."

"I know," she whispered, and quickly let him go. She was never a hugger and didn't really know what had come over her. "That was the most excitement I've had since … ever!" Embarrassment struck and she gave a nervous laugh, patting her hair to smooth it. "Let's go see if there's anything worth eating in the house, or if we just want to phone for pizza delivery. We have a choice in Crouch of pizza or nothing."

"I could go for pizza," he said.

"Me, too." She knew the number by heart and dialed it.

They took quick showers to wash away the grime and sweat of their hiking and fear as they waited for their dinner to be delivered.

Julia washed and dried her long hair and left it loose, and since it was already late, she put on her nightclothes and floor-length robe. When she entered the great room, she saw that Jean-Philippe had built a fire and made coffee. Also, he'd gotten dressed again in slacks and a pullover, but his feet were bare and his just washed hair was shiny and disheveled.

"You look all warm and cuddly," he said with a smile.

"I am." And you, she thought, look hot.

"Would you like some brandy?"

"Please," she said when she found her voice.

He poured them each a glass. They carried them to the sofa and sat. "*Santé, Julie*. You were very brave out there, and a good hiker."

"*Santé*," she said as they clinked their glasses and took a sip. "But I'm not brave, believe me. Although I do enjoy hiking and I often go camping."

"Who do you camp with?" he asked.

"No one."

"Isn't that dangerous?" He lifted a lock of her long hair, letting it slide like silk through his fingers.

Her breath caught even as she couldn't look away from him. "Maybe so, but I'm not giving it up."

"No, you wouldn't. You are fearless. You remind me of a dryad—a wood nymph." He put his glass down on the coffee table and then took hers and put it down as his arms circled her and drew her closer.

"And are you my lusty satyr?" she asked, even as her breath caught.

"Of course. And we should camp together sometime." His voice was a low rumble felt in the pit of her stomach.

Her pulse went into overdrive. A quick image of Jean-Philippe with her at night, under the stars ... sharing a tent ... flashed before her. This close, she could scarcely breathe as the man, even the scent of the soap and shampoo he'd used, enveloped her. She knew he wanted to kiss her—and knew she wanted him to.

But it was madness. Jean-Philippe with his money, his

upcoming trip to Spain—or was it Greenland?—his adventurous career. She was setting herself up for heartbreak if she allowed him to get close to her, and she'd spent way too many years protecting her heart to stop now.

As his arms tightened, she stiffened and drew back, her head high.

He shook his head. "*Julie,* what's wrong?

She faced the fireplace and shut her eyes. "I can't do this, Jean-Philippe."

"Am I so disagreeable to you?" he whispered.

Her eyes devoured him, his handsome features, the small laugh lines around his mouth, the hint of crows feet forming at the edges of his eyes, the masculine stubble over his cheeks and chin. She leaned forward, facing the fireplace. "No, quite the opposite. And that's the problem. The closer I get to you, when you leave, I'll ... I'll miss you." Her throat thickened and a longing so intense it was painful struck.

He lightly, gently rubbed her back. His tone was soft, husky. "But I'm here, now. I don't know when I'll leave."

"I know you don't," she said. She suspected he thought she was being silly—and definitely childish. She was a grown woman, and he was a very sexy man. She should take advantage of the two of them here, together ... tonight. She stood. It was too hard to think when close to him. She faced him again. "You had a brush with danger today. You could have been killed out there, so tonight you want to feel alive. But I'm not the person for that. Go to Mama's Folly. You'll find the companionship you seek."

She started for the foyer, to leave the room, but he caught her hand.

"I don't want to find 'companionship.' I want to be with you."

She met his eyes. "This is uncomfortable for me. And when things get uncomfortable, I leave—even if it's just to go upstairs to be alone. It's what I've always done, same as my mother and my father. It helps prevent awkward entanglements, okay? At some point, everyone leaves."

"Is it that you want to be alone, or are you afraid of staying here with me?"

Julia couldn't face him as she warred with herself, wanting to move closer to him, to take whatever he offered for as long as he was here. But she knew what the outcome would be and she couldn't bear the thought of how lonely she was going to feel when he left. She'd done it before—walked away from men who were growing interested in her. It was, she'd convinced herself, the smart thing to do. But at the same time, she was tired of feeling lonely. "Perhaps it's both," she whispered.

A knock sounded on the door.

"The pizza," Julia said breathlessly. She never knew she'd be so relieved to hear from a pizza delivery man. She stood, but then she heard the front door open.

She and Jean-Philippe locked eyes, confused. Smugglers wouldn't knock, but pizza delivery men wouldn't just enter...

Jean-Philippe stood and pulled her close, protectively, ready to run or fight just as she heard her sister Mallory's voice call out, "Hello? Julia?"

"Oh, my God!" Julia cried, her hand to her forehead as Mallory and Gunnar entered the great room. "You two scared the life out of us! Welcome back." Relieved, she overcame her usual hands-off demeanor and gave them quick hugs.

"We scared you? Why?" Mallory said, gawking at the state of dress of her sister and at the stranger who had been holding her, while Gunnar only commented with a "Hey, Jules." Then he, too, stared at Jean-Philippe.

Julia's cheeks reddened. Flustered, she said, "This is my—our —lodger, Jean-Philippe Fontaine. Jean-Philippe, this is my sister, Mallory, and her boyfriend, Gunnar McDermott."

"*Enchanté,*" Jean-Philippe said, holding out his hand.

Gunnar moved his cane to his left side as the two shook hands. "Nice to meet you, uh, John..."

"*Jean. Jean-Philippe.*"

Gunnar looked pained. "Is JP okay? If not, I do believe I will richly mangle it."

Jean-Philippe grinned. "I like JP. It's good."

"How was Montana?" Julia asked, tugging at her robe to smooth it.

"It was great," Mallory said, then gave Gunnar a quick smile. "And, I have to correct you. Gunnar isn't my boyfriend anymore." She raised her left hand.

Julia gasped, immediately focusing on the platinum band. Her sister hadn't been dubbed "the runaway bride" for nothing. "That cannot be a wedding ring."

"But it is," Mallory said.

Julia's head swiveled from Mallory to Gunnar who stood with a huge smile on his face. "Is this real or some kind of joke?"

He raised his left hand. "If so, the joke's on me."

"Oh, my! I never thought I'd see this day. Congratulations, you two!" Julia gave them each another quick hug. "I can't believe, Mallory, that you finally came to your senses!"

Jean-Philippe walked over to Julia and put his arm around her waist. "It sounds as if congratulations are in order."

"Thank you," Mallory said, clearly stunned as her eyes jumped between Jean-Philippe and her sister.

"We appreciate it," Gunnar said.

"We were sharing some brandy," Jean-Philippe said. "Perhaps a toast?"

Gunnar looked ready to accept, but Mallory shook her head. "It's late, and we still have to stop by Gunnar's parents' house to tell them the news," Mallory said. "This way his mother will stop looking at me as if I'm the worst woman alive since Jezebel for 'leading her son on,' but then refusing to marry him."

"So, what convinced you?" Julia asked.

Mallory looked at Gunnar to explain. He put his arm around her shoulders. "It took a while, but I eventually figured out Mallory was more spooked by the whole wedding thing than by actually being married. Then, I remembered hearing about common-law marriages in the Old West." His gaze went to Jean-Philippe. "In the early days of the country, there weren't a lot of Justices of the Peace around so many of the states came up with a way for people to legally marry themselves. No one else needed to be there, no ceremonies, nothing. We just had to hold ourselves out to the public as husband and wife, and feel in our hearts that we are as bound together by love as any two people could ever be. And so we are."

"That's all, to legally marry?" Jean-Philippe asked, his eyes wide. "It's incredible."

"In Montana and a few other states." Gunnar smiled at Jean-Philippe's astonishment. "That was the only way I could get this lovely woman to become my bride."

Mallory looked at Gunnar. "That's right," she said, her arms around his waist. "But, just to make sure everyone—like Gunnar's mom—knows it's true, I'm going to send for an affidavit from Montana to prove it."

He did a double-take. "You're kidding me. I thought you didn't want any formalities."

"It's just a paper that we sign and have notarized." She grinned. "That, I can do."

"Thank you." He gave her a quick kiss.

Mallory faced Julia. "We'd better get going, but I just wanted you to know that we're back."

"I'm so glad," Julia said. "Glad for both of you."

Gunnar turned to leave, but Mallory stopped him. "How's the cabin treating you?" she asked Julia.

"Well, let's just say it's been interesting," Julia admitted with a quick glance at Jean-Philippe. "But there's nothing to worry about. I'm getting the hang of it better and better each day."

"She is an excellent hostess," Jean-Philippe said.

"I can tell," Mallory said with a grin as her eyebrows rose. "Anyway, I really appreciate you coming here for me, Jules. And we'll figure out what to do with her soon."

"Her?"

"The cabin."

"The Donnelly House, you mean," Julia stated.

Mallory frowned. "Oh? Where did that name come from? It's rather stuffy, don't you think?"

"Let's go, Mal. I think we're interrupting." Gunnar eased her toward the door. "Besides, you two start talking about the cabin and it'll be midnight before we get home."

"We'll talk soon," Mallory said. "Good to meet you, Jean-Philippe."

Jean-Philippe and Gunnar said their goodbyes as Julia watched her baby sister leave the house.

Jean-Philippe looked at Julia. "They are a couple the ghosts helped bring together, no?"

"So it seems," she said.

He nodded. "They did good. The ghosts found true love for both your sisters. I think they will for you someday as well."

"No, not me," Julia said. "I think that's an area I'm like my mother. They failed her, too. But she made the mistake of constantly searching for the right man. I'm smarter than that."

He seemed to ponder that a moment. "I see. But have you ever thought that the ghosts found a true love for your mother and she rejected him for some reason, and that's why she was never happy?"

"A lot of people have thought that. But I've never heard a word of who that very special man might have been, so I think it's that some Donnelly women are lucky in love, and some of us just aren't."

The pizza was delivered soon. After dinner, Jean-Philippe drove into Crouch where both his cell phone and Internet would work to report to his team all that had happened in the forest. It was past midnight when Julia, alone in her bedroom, heard his truck pull onto the driveway.

CHAPTER 15

A freshly baked tray of scones awaited Jean-Philippe the next morning. Julia proudly stood by them as he entered the great room. She'd gotten up early enough to use a recipe Carly had sent her. For some reason, she wanted to show off her baking skills. Or, more accurately, to find out if she had any baking skills to show off. They not only came out just fine, but were also ready for an eight a.m. breakfast.

Jean-Philippe sounded appropriately impressed as he grabbed two of them plus coffee on his way to the forest. There, he'd meet with his team to show where the trap had been found and to see the state of the ATV.

After he left, Julia cleaned up the cabin, as was becoming her routine, and then headed to Crouch's grocery store to shop for the next morning's fresh fruit, as well as some wine and snack foods.

At the grocery, her cell service came back to life, and she discovered five missed calls from Mallory. She phoned her sister back. "I saw you've been calling, but no messages. Is everything okay?"

"I want to know all about Jean-Philippe," Mallory said. "He is so good-looking! What is he doing at the cabin? And what's going on between the two of you?"

"There's nothing going on. We were dressed the way you saw us because we'd been running through the mountains for hours and needed showers. That's all."

"Why were you running through mountains?"

"It's a long story. You ask too many questions, and I'm busy."

"Wait, Jules."

"There's nothing between us. Not now. Not ever. And he's leaving for Spain or heaven-only-knows where very soon, so forget it."

"I'm sorry to hear that," Mallory said.

"Well, I'm not," Julia firmly stated. "Now, I've got to get some groceries. Talk to you later." With that, she hung up without even waiting for Mallory's goodbye.

She found herself fretting about Mallory's nosy questions all the way through the grocery store. Once back at the cabin, after putting away the groceries, she decided the best way to forget about Mallory *and* her confused feelings about Jean-Philippe was to gather her paints and head for the river.

She had expected to be alone when she reached it, but was in for a surprise. "You're here," she said to Luke with a smile. "I've missed you."

He had propped up his easel and was now painting a portrait of his former nurse in oils. "And I've missed you."

She stepped behind him and admired his painting. Questions filled her mind, but she hesitated to ask any of them.

"I went to the forest with my lodger yesterday," she explained after a while. "He's a French scientist studying raptors. It's all quite interesting. He was fascinated that we saw a gyrfalcon here—the beautiful arctic bird. Would you like to meet him?"

"No."

The curt answer surprised her. "Are you sure? He's also intrigued by the sketch you drew of your nurse."

"If he's at the cabin looking for love, he'll have to look elsewhere. She's married."

Julia debated how much to tell him. "That's not why he's here. I think the only thing he loves at the moment are falcons."

"That's too bad. After what happened with your sisters meeting their true loves at the cabin, I couldn't help but think that now you're there, and he's there..." His eyebrows raised.

"Don't be silly! I'm quite content with the way things are in my life. I'm a loner. Always have been."

"Oh?" He sounded skeptical.

"I mean, I've seen a lot of really troubled relationships, and nothing—I mean nothing—in my past would lead me to believe any relationship I'm in wouldn't be a mess."

His mouth wrinkled. "Really?"

"My mother's life was a textbook example of how not to fall in love."

"I'm sorry that's what you learned from her." He seemed to study her a moment before adding, "I've always heard she should have simply married Mike Halkonen. She really loved him, and that was probably why she was never happy with anyone else she married."

An electric shock-like jolt hit Julia at those words as time seemed to stand still. *The print shop owner? Roxanne and the print shop owner?* No way. Roxanne always chose men who were tall and handsome and either had money or talked a good game about how they'd get it. "Mike Halkonen? No, impossible. He's not her type at all."

"You know him?"

Her breathing quickened as flashes came to her of the way Mike—Miika—Halkonen had studied her ... Miika with his whitish blond hair, his cobalt eyes, even his small stature ... and of the way he had reacted when he learned of Roxanne's death. Her head felt light.

"I heard," Luke continued, "he was the reason she came back here each summer—to see him and to show him how successful she'd become. And then, a few years back, after he married someone else, she never returned to the cabin again."

Julia's head was spinning. She went over to the log and sat. A picture filled her mind of Mike's son. She had thought he looked familiar to her. Suddenly she knew why. She saw many of his features, his hair, the shape of his mouth, the form of his eyes, in the mirror each day.

"Oh, my God," Julia pressed her hand to her mouth, her mind reeled and she couldn't help but wonder why, when she had a choice of print shops to go to, something had caused her, with Jean-Philippe's help, to choose that one. Was it pure chance or was something more at work here? She wanted to tell Jean-Philippe about this, to see what he thought.

"What's wrong, Julia?" Luke asked.

"Why didn't you tell me this before?" she demanded.

"You never spoke of your mother before. And ... and I thought you knew."

He set up his easel and concentrated on painting, not saying anything more to her. One thought after the other raced through her head. But most of all, she wondered if Hugh Perrin had known Mike Halkonen. Was that why his marriage to Roxanne had been such a disaster? And if he did, as Julia grew older, Hugh must have come to believe he wasn't her father. After all, she looked nothing like her tall, handsome, red-haired father. Had she been a constant reminder to him that his marriage to Roxanne had been a sham? Was that why, after he left for Australia, contact with him grew less and less until it fizzled out completely?

"How did you know about Roxanne and Mike Halkonen?" she asked finally.

He put down his paint brush. "I'm not sure. It was one of those things I've always known. I think a lot of people knew. From what I'd heard, they met when they were teenagers, and everyone thought they'd marry. Of course, Roxanne—I've heard—had ambition and Mike apparently didn't fit into her plans."

Julia shut her eyes a moment. She could see it all playing out before her. Roxanne had been a "star" in the area. Her parents, Julia's grandparents, had lived in Boise but spent most of their free time, weekends and vacations, at the cabin. Roxanne had loved Garden Valley and had a lot of friends there. "If she loved Mike Halkonen, why did she marry Hugh Perrin?"

"I've never heard why your mother did a lot of the things she did," Luke said. "Apparently, she left Garden Valley one summer and didn't come back for a couple of years. When she finally did, she was married to someone else and had a toddler. I guess that was you."

"She always came back in July," Julia murmured. "Every year."

"July … and she named you Julia," he mused. "I wonder what that means?"

"A coincidence, I'm sure!" She spat out the words even as she was trying to figure out its meaning.

She wasn't born in July; her birthday was in April. She counted back the months and even before she did, she knew what she'd find. She was very likely conceived in July. Had Roxanne spent that July in Garden Valley with Mike Halkonen, the man she apparently had loved?

Julia never knew exactly when Roxanne and Hugh Perrin married—or even how long they were engaged. Hugh Perrin never would talk about it with her. She couldn't help but suspect Roxanne had married him knowing she was carrying Mike Halkonen's child.

Mike was ... he was a plain guy, but Hugh Perrin looked like someone a star of stage or screen would be married to.

So many thoughts, so many possibilities went through Julia's mind.

She wondered if she dared to confront Miika Halkonen. Why hadn't he said anything to her? He had to know. Didn't he?

"What do you think?" Luke's words interrupted her thoughts.

It took her a moment to come back to the present and realize Luke was talking about the portrait he was painting.

She walked over to it. He was a fine artist. The sketch had been a work of art, but now, with oils, he'd captured the woman beautifully. Looking at it, Julia was certain Luke had lost his heart to his nurse. No one could remember anyone in such detail or sketch her so magnificently if he didn't love her.

But was she looking at a portrait of his nurse ... or was it a portrait of Claire Dumont, the older Lucas Donnelly's nurse? "It's wonderful," she said. "Were you in an American hospital when you met her?"

"No. I'd been transferred to a French one."

Of course you were.

"I'm pleased with the way the picture is coming along," he admitted.

"Well you should be," she murmured. As she looked at his canvas, noting more than ever the similarity in style between it and the Elijah Donnelly portrait, a coldness rippled through her. On top of the revelation about Mike Halkonen, it was more than she could deal with.

Luke and whoever—or whatever—he was, was particularly more than she could deal with. She backed away from him.

"I'm afraid you've tapped into a love I didn't even realize I had," he said, his eyes never leaving his work. "It feels good to go back to it."

"I'm glad," Julia murmured, and then forced herself to ask. "Tell me, does … does your nurse have a name?"

"Of course." He gave her an odd look, an almost defiant stare as he said, "Her name is Claire."

She tossed her paints into the easel case and slammed it shut.

"What's wrong, Julia?" Luke asked.

"I've got to leave. I'm sorry." She didn't even look at him as she hurried back to the cabin.

———

As soon as Jean-Philippe's meeting with representatives from the U.S. Fish and Wildlife Service, Idaho Fish and Game, and the Peregrine Foundation ended, he returned to the cabin. There was some suggestion that since the smugglers might now know they were being watched, they might try to find out who it was watching them. Jean-Philippe and the others were told to keep an eye out for anything strange that afternoon. Things could become dangerous.

He entered the cabin expecting to find Julia on the sofa or dining table with her laptop working on small "gigs" as a graphic designer to bring in a few extra dollars. But she wasn't there.

His nerves turned raw as an awful dread filled his mind. What if the smugglers recognized them? No, he told himself. Julia must have gone down to the river, that's all. But then he saw her portable easel propped against a wall near the kitchen.

"Julia?" he called, hearing the urgency in his own voice as he ran to the stairs, hoping she was in the bedroom. No reply. Could she be asleep? He went upstairs and flung open the door to her room.

He was surprised at how sparse it was. No pictures. A stack of books about graphic design and marketing. Nothing in the least bit personal. It was as if she had purposefully suppressed any indication of who she was and how she felt about things. But then he saw a canvas leaning against a wall. The back was toward him. He went over to it and picked it up.

It was a painting of the river near the cabin, but as he had never seen it. It was filled with mist and mystery, beautiful, done with purples and grays giving an air of intrigue. It was, he had to admit, pure Julia, difficult to see clearly, subtle, yet alluring, a place—a person—he found himself inexplicably drawn to.

It also showed him why he should stay away from her. There was a darkness there, a sadness. A sense that he could get sucked up into that strange void filled him. She'd been smart to rebuff his advances last night. What had he been thinking? He didn't need a complicated person like her in his life.

He'd decided to take the position he'd been offered in Greenland. He could go to Spain anytime, and Greenland offered a chance for research that would be welcomed in his field as more peregrine falcons seem to be moving farther north in Greenland, trying to take over the nesting grounds of the original inhabitants, the gyrfalcons. It was interesting that as much as gyrfalcons traveled during the course of winter, heading south for food, they returned to the same nesting grounds year after years. Home, so to speak.

He liked that about them. It was strange, when he thought about it, that he didn't have such a home to return to. The closest thing had been Grandmere's apartment in Paris. But after her death he couldn't bear to go there, to be among all her belongings, and not see her. So he'd sold everything.

And now, he was completely free.

He put the painting back, just the way he'd found it.

Julia … she had to be all right.

He raced downstairs. Maybe she'd gone for a walk? Before leaving the cabin, he decided to try the back porch and even the garage. He opened the French doors to the porch and stopped, relieved and thankful. She sat wearing a heavy jacket, a cup of tea at her side. "You're here!" he exclaimed.

She turned sad eyes on him. "I am. Why?"

He saw how unhappy she looked. "I was worried when I didn't see you inside. The smugglers—"

"They have no idea who we are, I'm sure," she murmured, then stared out at the orchard.

He took a seat on the bench with her. "Are you all right?"

Her expression grew confused and guarded. She didn't answer.

"What's wrong?" He saw her blinking, as if trying to hold back tears. Seeing this strong woman so troubled made him ache for her, made him want to let her know that whatever it was, she didn't have to face it alone.

But instead of answering, she shook her head, then turned her face farther from his watchful eyes.

"Please, I know it's something." He took her hand, but in typical Julia fashion, she pulled it free.

"My neighbor, Luke ... his nurse's name was Claire. That's what he just told me."

"What? Your neighbor?" He couldn't believe thinking about Luke had caused so much sadness in her. She, again, didn't trust him enough to tell him what was really wrong. But then ... why should she? "Impossible."

"Don't pretend, Jean-Philippe." Her voice was harsh, angry, broken. "You knew it all along."

Where was this coming from? He stood. "I *knew* it? What did I know? That Luke's nurse's name was Claire? Is that what you're saying? Tell me, how could I know such a thing?"

Her hands clenched. "What are you up to? Who are you really?" Again, she turned away from him, rejecting him. And it hurt.

He took hold of her upper arms and made her look at him as he stood over her. "You know who I am, Julia. I've been nothing but honest with you."

"But nothing makes sense," she insisted, pushing him away. "If you didn't know Luke before you came here, how does he know your great-grandparents' story?"

"I don't know," Jean-Philippe said, standing straight now and running his hands through his hair.

"It's crazy," she insisted. "So much is crazy! And..." She covered her face with her hands.

He sat down beside her once more. "Is it?" he asked, his voice gentle now. "There is a simple answer to all this."

She glared at him. "No."

"Has anyone but you ever seen your neighbor?" he asked.

"I don't know."

"I would suspect not."

"Are you saying I imagined him? That I'm making all this up? If so, who drew the sketch of Claire Dumont that you saw in my notebook?"

His expression hardened. "There are only two possibilities. You've grown up with stories of the ghosts, you've looked at Lucas Donnelly's portrait of his father for years, and you, too, are an artist."

"No!" She walked to the porch railing, gripped it, and leaned out toward the orchard. "That's outrageous! Besides, I've never seen Claire Dumont until you showed me her picture!"

He leaned back against the bench. "I believe you. Which means the other possibility must be the correct one."

She faced him once more. A shiver seemed to go through her body. "My neighbor is *not* a ghost or a figment of my imagination!"

"The best way to know what's going on is for me to meet your neighbor," Jean-Philippe said. "And you need to be there so you'll know I'm not lying to you."

"Maybe. All I know is, I'm sick to death of family secrets! Old and new!" With that, she went into the cabin, slamming the French door so hard he thought for sure some of the glass panes would crack.

For dinner, Julia made a green salad and spaghetti with a jar of store-bought red sauce. She said nothing to Jean-Philippe, but was making enough for two in case he wanted to join her.

To her surprise, Jean-Philippe saw what she was doing, and pulled some hamburger meat, onion, and parsley from the refrigerator, and used them to silently cook meatballs, adding a number of spices from the spice rack to both the meatballs and the store-bought sauce.

She felt bad about the way she'd treated him out on the deck. She didn't really think he and Luke had plotted out some grand scheme to fool her about Claire Dumont. Although she couldn't, yet, accept what Jean-Philippe was suggesting—that Luke was, in fact, some manifestation of Lucas Donnelly.

The two cooked in an awkward silence. When they finally sat down to eat, she was amazed at how delicious the meal turned out, thanks to Jean-Philippe's intervention.

"Would you like some wine, *Julie?*" Jean-Philippe asked.

"Wine sounds good," she said.

He opened a bottle of red and poured them each a glass. "Tonight, we need to forget about families, ghosts, strange paintings, and the two of us arguing about them," he said, and then held out his glass toward her. "*Santé.*"

"I agree." She clinked her glass to his. "*Santé.*"

As they ate, Jean-Philippe told her about his meetings with the other biologists and government officials about the falcon trap they'd found the day before. She found it all quite interesting, but wasn't in the least pleased to hear that Jean-Philippe had been warned that the two of them might not be safe if the smugglers were able to see who they were, and fear they have some proof of the smugglers' identity. But he was sure the smugglers couldn't tell who they were with their heavy winter jackets and head-coverings.

The meal over, they cleaned up the kitchen together. "I think, tonight," Jean-Philippe began—and Julia could hear a hint of caution in his voice, "tonight we deserve for ourselves to do something fun."

"Fun? You've got to be kidding," Julia said. "I'm in no mood for fun."

"That's because you need cheering up." Jean-Philippe gave her one of his infectious smiles. She honestly didn't know why he was suddenly being so nice to her. She wanted to find an ulterior motive, but couldn't. "I'd like you to teach me to line dance."

Her mouth fell open. "What? You want to go to Mama's Folly now?"

"No. Look." He went to his jacket and pulled a cassette tape from the pocket. "I found this in a shop after my meeting in Horseshoe Bend. The owner said it had all the best songs."

She took the tape he excitedly waved at her. "Oh, my! Well, I do love Waylon. His voice is gorgeous. And these are classics. 'Mama, Don't Let Your Babies Grow Up to be Cowboys,' 'Luckenbach, Texas.' Ah, here's one that's popular for line dancing—'Good-Hearted Woman.'"

Jean-Philippe got them each a beer. "Then let's do this. We deserve a laugh or two, and I suspect you will find me trying to line dance to be very funny."

"I don't know …"

"All those steps that the fellow was calling out like 'grapevine' and 'jazz square' and many strange words. I need to learn them."

"You do?" She couldn't help but smile.

"*Mais, oui!*"

That caused a laugh. "So, you were paying attention to us out there dancing!"

"Of course. You looked quite cute."

She shook her head. "Cute? No way. But all right, I'll teach you just so you'll stop bugging me. We'll do the electric slide. It's really basic, and lots of people do it." She showed him the steps, one by one, and he followed.

"That's quite easy," he said.

They did it facing all four directions, slowly. "Okay, let's go through it one more time."

"Why? I'm not a child. It is very simple. Put on the music! Let's dance."

She raised her eyebrows. "As you wish." She put the tape into the cassette player and rushed to his side. "… five, six, seven, eight, grapevine left!"

He joined her in one direction, then the other, but soon, his steps fell apart, and he ended up scrambling and going in the wrong direction. She couldn't help but laugh at the astonished look on his face. After a second beer, he said, "Okay, let's try it again."

And again.

Soon, they were both laughing hard. "It's not symmetrical!" he complained. "You should do the same thing on both sides!"

"Why? That would be boring!"

"Oh. Maybe, so." He frowned.

"As for what to do with your arms, if you want to look like a badass cowboy, you can hook your thumbs in your belt."

He did it. "That, I like. But I have a better idea about what to do with my arms." Saying that, he wrapped them around her.

The heat he'd worked up while line dancing radiated off him. In that moment, he was everything she'd ever wanted. She'd resisted him before, but tonight, all resistance was gone. Her hands slid up along his chest until her arms circled his neck. The scent of the outdoors and sunshine on his body mixed with the beer they'd been drinking. But more than anything she was aware of the way he looked at her, the desire in his eyes. She was aware of every inch of him.

He drew her closer until she met his kisses with her own.

She found him attractive, not only physically, but she'd come to know he was a good man, loyal, caring, and with a heart she admired.

And he was a really good kisser. A long time passed before she realized how completely she had melted into his arms, and how much she loved the sensations that rippled through her body at his touch.

Only the smallest semblance of rationality stopped her from making a complete fool of herself with him, and she drew back. "That music can touch the heart and make people do uncharacteristic things," she said, hating how revealing the breathless quality was in her voice.

His eyes slowly captured every inch of her face, causing her to grow increasingly uneasy until he said, "Or, perhaps, it allows people to do what they've wanted to for a long time."

"That's also possible," she admitted before she walked away from him, turned off the cassette player, and with a quick "goodnight," rushed upstairs to her bedroom.

CHAPTER 16

Julia could scarcely sleep that night. She couldn't stop thinking about her strong reaction to Jean-Philippe—to everything about him from his work to help capture smugglers to his joy at simple things like line dancing and good food, to his interest in his family's history, and most of all to the love of that family that made him the man he was now. That very attractive, fun, trustworthy man. And her growing feelings about him, more than anything, scared her.

But then, when she flopped over to her other side in hopes of stopping such thoughts, her mind dredged up visions of confronting Miika or Mike or whatever he called himself, and of all the things she would like to say to him.

He had to have known about her, had to have known he was her father. Yet, he didn't want her. But then, why should he? No one else did.

An old memory suddenly struck. She was quite young, holding the hand of her sister Carly outside Miss Sandie's Ice Cream Parlor in Crouch as they waited for Roxanne to buy them ice cream cones. A man got out of his truck, looked straight at her, and all but froze there in the street. She remembered thinking his hair was almost white—like hers. She wondered if people called him a "towhead" the way they did her. She was too young to know the term and thought people were saying her head looked like a toe, which she hated.

But then Roxanne came out of the shop, saw the man, and hustled the kids into her car.

Julia had forgotten that until now. But thinking back, she couldn't help but suspect that man had been Miika Halkonen.

Most of all, she couldn't help but wonder what the big picture was here. Somehow, everything that was happening around her seemed to be connected. She wondered if, from the moment she first met Luke, all of this had been set in motion. If Jean-Philippe hadn't come to the cabin, led here by the story about the ghosts, if Luke hadn't made a drawing of Claire Dumont in her sketch book, if Luke hadn't told her about Miika Halkonen and her mother, and if Jean-Philippe hadn't brought Claire Dumont's diary with him … then her life would haven't been turned on its head. And she'd still be the person she was when she first moved to the cabin from Bend, Oregon.

But all that did happen, and she was no longer the same.

In fact, right now, she wasn't all that sure who she was.

And so her night continued, tossing and turning, from Jean-Philippe to Miika to Luke and back again.

When she finally rolled out of bed, exhausted, she headed downstairs and made coffee.

She had forgotten to pick up fresh pastries at the grocery, but she had bought a package of frozen cinnamon rolls for a time like this. She put them in the oven and hoped for the best.

They were almost ready when Jean-Philippe came downstairs. "*Bonjour, Julie.*"

The memory of his kisses underscored the way her pulse sped up at the sight of him. He, too, seemed unnerved, and they circled each other a moment, but then he boldly strode to her side and kissed her on the cheek. "What is the heavenly aroma that wakes me this morning?"

The kiss surprised her, but it was as if the dam broke. She realized that by doing it, he had acknowledged a change in their relationship, not an awkward one, but one they would need to work out in the days to come, before he left for parts unknown.

She could see why he liked falcons. They swoop in, create a bit of havoc, then fly off again. Just like Jean-Philippe.

"Let's see if the cinnamon rolls are ready." She opened the oven door to find the rolls golden brown.

Jean-Philippe frowned at the cream cheese icing. He decided on toast with his coffee. Julia realized he didn't have much of a sweet tooth, but she loved the rolls. They were much better than PopTarts.

As they ate, she received a call on the cabin's landline that her print job was ready. It wasn't Miika who called—the voice was way too young. She guessed it might be her half-brother's voice.

Half-brother ... what a strange feeling that gave her.

How, she wondered, would that young man feel about all this? The call gave her an opening to tell Jean-Philippe about Miika Halkonen, but she couldn't bring herself to do it. Instead, when he asked who had called, she said it was a wrong number. The look he gave her told her he knew she was lying.

As he headed off to the forest, leaving her to wonder if he'd ever invite her to go with him again, she cleaned the cabin, held off phone calls from Carly about her sexy boarder—obviously, Mallory had filled her in—finished a small gig job, and last of all, continued to work on the cabin's website.

She knew she needed to do some advertising to bring customers to the cabin, but she was in no mood to do it. She thought about going to the river to see Luke, but she didn't yet know what to say to him. Everything was simply too strange.

So she stuck with her familiar, non-judgmental, uncomplicated computer. At five p.m. she heard a knock on the door. Could it be someone looking for a room? She should want it to be a customer, but at the same time, she didn't think she could handle any more disruption.

She opened the door to see a round-faced, middle-aged fellow wearing a starched blue-and-gray Western-cut shirt, a braided-leather bolo tie with a turquoise and silver slide, creased blue jeans, and cowboy boots. She didn't know the rodeo had come to town.

"Are you Julia Perrin?" he asked.

She hesitated, but then said a slow, "Yes."

"I'm Ryan Salzburg. We have an appointment."

Oh, no! He was the fellow she'd hired to help her learn to become a good bed-and-breakfast hostess. She'd forgotten all about him.

"Excuse my clothes," he quickly added, perhaps in response to the way she was scowling at him. "I'm going to a line-dancing class after we finish here."

Her mouth downturned. "There seems to be a lot of that going around. Come on inside."

He looked a bit confused by her statement, but entered the cabin. He stopped at the entrance to the great room. "I must say, this log cabin certainly has beautiful modern conveniences." He gave a nod toward the kitchen.

"For the most part," she said. "But it's small. And the furniture in the bedrooms is pretty dated."

"New mattresses, I hope?" he said with a wink.

No, he hadn't just done that, she told herself.

"I didn't have a choice." She folded her arms. "Over the years, the mice got more use out of them than anyone else. That's why I've got two cats."

As if on cue, Pumpkin and Otis—who had not only become friends but actually hung out together—strolled into the room and sat, side-by-side, staring at the man.

He looked startled. "Oh, well. Why don't we sit and discuss what you'd like to learn?" He seemed to study the sofa a long moment, as if looking for signs of mice living inside it.

She took the easy chair farthest from him.

"So," he began, "you're operating this cabin as a bed and breakfast, and your only problem is … what?"

"How to make the guests not only feel comfortable, but to want to come back."

"And what about you?" he asked. "Do you like having guests here in this relatively small space? I'd imagine you need to share a bathroom with them."

"I hate it, but it is what it is."

"But you hate it," he said, giving her an intense look. "So, if this isn't what you want to be doing, why are you doing it?"

She hadn't expected an interrogation from the guy and had no patience for one. "Look, Ryan, all I want is to learn how to make the guests comfortable. Tell me what to do. Do I simply need to smile more? If so, I will. But let's get this show on the road."

"I see." He cleared his throat. "Well, you certainly have no problem making your wishes clear."

He then handed her a brochure of the services he offered, mostly in Boise, from a simple plan to a platinum plan that included six months of on-call assistance.

She looked over the cost of the plans and found them crazy. "I don't want to sign up for any of these. It's not like I'm running a hotel here. Like I said on the phone, all I want"—she stabbed the arm of the easy chair with her forefinger—"is to learn to make customers feel welcome. Period."

His eyes widened a moment, then he smiled. "I think I see the problem. You don't need a customer relations coach, you need coaching on how to make small talk with a total stranger."

"What? Small talk? Nonsense!" She sat back and glowered at him.

"Is it?" he asked. "What if we just sit here and chat? What would you say to me?"

Her eyes rolled. "How should I know!"

"Exactly! Small talk will put your guests at ease."

She thought about what he was saying. "Maybe," she mumbled.

"I usually have to start with a lesson in self-confidence and speaking up. But you seem to have no problem in that area. And you don't need to eye your customers as if they're potential robbers who are going to make off with the family silver—as you did me when you looked over the brochure I gave you."

"I don't do that!" she stated.

"Yes, you did. In fact, you're doing it now, and I'm the guy who's here to help you."

She again folded her arms. She added a hard glare in case he hadn't picked up on her mood.

He stood up. "Let do a little role-playing. I'm your customer. You're going to greet me at the door. We'll do this over and over until you greet me in a way that makes me feel welcome."

"No. I hate role-playing," Julia said, still seated.

"Come on. You can do it." He walked over to her, took her hands, and pulled her to her feet. "Now, I'm the customer. What's the first thing you say to me?"

She pulled her hands free. "I'd like you to leave."

"Very funny. You need to greet me! Say, 'Hello. Welcome to whatever-you-call-this-place.'"

"This place is called the Donnelly House," she said, hands on hips. "And I'd like you to leave."

"Come on, Julia. You can't mean that." He smiled and, stepping closer, waggled his finger at her. "You're a challenge and I like that. I like it a lot. In fact, I'd like to get to know you better —if it's okay with you."

She refused to move away, but she couldn't stop herself from bending back from him. He didn't get the message because he puffed out his chest. "In fact, I can't help but wonder if you're free—"

"Ahem!" The sound came from behind her. She turned to see Jean-Philippe leaning against the wall by the entry to the great room. He looked comfortable, as if he'd been there for some time listening. At her glance, he straightened and began to stroll toward them.

"Jean-Philippe, I didn't hear you come in," she said, then faced Ryan. "This is my lodger, Jean-Philippe Fontaine. This is Ryan Salzburg. He's helping me learn to be a good hostess to my guests."

"Oh, is that what he's doing?" Jean-Philippe asked, his eyebrows raised. "Good to meet you, Mr. Salzburg." He held out his hand.

Ryan shook it, looking uncomfortable. "You, too. Hope you're enjoying your stay here."

"Very much. Miss Julia is already an excellent hostess. I am surprised you think she needs any lessons."

"I'm sure she is, but there's always more to learn," Ryan said. "Excuse us, please." He then turned his back on Jean-Philippe and addressed Julia. "Shall we continue with your lesson? I'll teach you everything you need to know about being nice to people, and... *Hey! What's going on?*"

Ryan's bolo tie suddenly lifted from his shirt and started to pull him toward the door. He flailed his arms, unable to stop the leather cords from dragging him along at a pace so fast he was all but running. In mere seconds, he crossed the great room and the foyer. Then, as if by its own volition, the front door swung open, Ryan went through it, and it shut behind him.

The deadbolt snapped all by itself into the "lock" position.

Jean-Philippe stood rooted to the spot.

Julia watched with her mouth hanging open, and then she dropped onto the sofa.

What she just saw was impossible.

Jean-Philippe took his place on the sofa beside Julia and stared at her. "What in the world was that?"

Julia couldn't speak, but simply shook her head.

CHAPTER 17

"I think it's best if we forget what we just saw," Julia said, trying to control the quiver in her voice, the way her hands had begun to shake.

"Hold my hands," Jean-Philippe took hers and held them tight, helping to calm her. His fingers were much longer than hers and his grip was firm. "It'll be all right. They aren't dangerous."

"They?" she whispered.

"You know who I mean. Come here." He put his arms around her and held her against his chest, her head on his shoulder. They sat silently for a long time.

"Why aren't you afraid?" she whispered.

"Of what? A presence? The way they scared the odious Crystal, and booted out—or maybe I should say 'bolo-ed out'—the equally obnoxious consultant you hired, they seem to be doing a good thing. And they are my relatives. Maybe even my great-grandfather."

"I don't see how you can speak so calmly of such madness," she whispered.

"Why not? No one besides you would believe me anyway," Jean-Philippe added. The two remained unmoving on the sofa.

"True enough," she murmured. She was enjoying being in his arms a little too much and sat upright. "And Ryan Salzburg won't say a word unless he wants his customers to think he's gone past the limits of lunacy."

"But the expression on his face surely was funny," Jean-Philippe said with a lopsided grin.

"It was." Julia also smiled. "Sort of like when Crystal ran all over screaming like a certifiable whack job about a dead mouse."

They started to laugh, but just as suddenly, both their smiles vanished.

"Have we both gone quite mad?" Jean-Philippe asked.

"You're part of this family, too," she said. "You tell me."

Pumpkin jumped up onto the coffee table and batted Ryan Salzburg's brochure until it fell onto the floor.

They stared at it in silence a moment, then Jean-Philippe spoke. "You haven't mentioned Luke in a while. Have you seen him recently?"

"Yesterday," she said, steeling herself to finally tell him all Luke had said about Mike Halkonen.

But Jean-Philippe spoke first. "You should ask him if he's willing to meet me."

She sucked in her breath. "I did, but I'm afraid he said no."

Jean-Philippe's posture went rigid, his expression pinched. "I must talk to him."

"How? Do you plan to hide at the riverbank and jump out when you see him?"

"If that's what it takes! I say we go to his house."

"As I told you, I don't know where he lives."

"If he's a neighbor as he claims, and he walks to the riverbank, he can't be that far away. You said he walks down the dirt road in front of the cabin to go home. So let's take it and see what we can find."

"All right," she said. "But it's too late to do anything like that. It's already dark out."

"We do it tomorrow." He looked hard at her. "What else is troubling you? I've felt since last night that there's something you aren't telling me."

She didn't know how to bring herself to open up to him. What was she supposed to say? That she just found out her whole life had been a lie? That the man who had reluctantly raised her wasn't even her father? And her real father didn't want to acknowledge her? "It's nothing."

"I suspected by the stubborn look on your face that you'd refuse to tell me."

"Stubborn?" she exclaimed.

"So, there's only one thing to do. We're getting out of here. This cabin is nice, but right now, with the ghosts here as well, it feels claustrophobic. We're going to Mama's Folly for dinner and also because I want to give the dance steps you taught me a try."

She looked horrified. "No, no, no."

"Yes, yes, yes." He stood. "You spend too much time worrying. Take it from Grandmere. When the world goes crazy, the best thing to do is dance."

"Dance?"

"Grapevine! Coaster step! And stomp!" At that, he stomped on the floor.

She looked heavenward and shook her head. "Fine. Let's get it over with."

Julia was a nervous wreck. It's not a date, she told herself. So why be nervous? But it felt like a date to the point where she even dressed nicer than usual. Not a dress. She didn't go that far, but since Jean-Philippe was interested in line dancing in public she put on snug, black, boot-cut jeans, a much-loved pair of tooled, high-heeled cowboy boots, and a fitted Western shirt. She even left her hair loose, letting it cascade down her back.

Jean-Philippe jumped to his feet as she stepped into the great room. "You look *tres belle*. Like a beautiful Annie Oakley."

"I don't think so," she said with a laugh.

"It's true." His gaze drifted over her. "You should wear clothes your size more often."

Her eyebrows rose, and it was on the tip of her tongue to tell him what she thought of that suggestion. On the other hand, she had to admit his compliments made her feel good. And maybe she did overdo it a bit with the baggy duds. "Maybe so," she admitted with a smile.

He took her arm and led her out to his truck. "Can we go shopping for cowboy boots for me? I like the way they look."

"I think I can find the time one of these days."

They were soon at the restaurant. Mama's Folly was lively as ever. "Want to get a drink before we sit down to eat?" Julia asked. She hoped a beer would help calm her nerves.

"Yes, an apéritif sounds good," he said.

The bartender stood in front of them. "What'll it be?"

She knew her nervousness was way past the ability of beer to help. "Tequila. Straight up."

Jean-Philippe did a double-take, then said, "Same."

They each downed two shots before she felt she might have the courage, or sheer chutzpah, to go out there and join the line-dancers. When the strong beat of "A Little Less Talk and a Lot More Action" brought people to the floor doing the electric slide, Julia took Jean-Philippe's hand. "Show time."

She had a lot more fun on the dance floor with Jean-Philippe than the group she'd been with last week. And when the slow, romantic, "Feels So Right," began, without asking, without saying a word, Jean-Philippe took her into his arms.

She stiffened for only a moment, but he held her close, his head to hers, and she let herself ease against him, loving the way she felt with him. It was all about the tequila, she told herself, not the man in her arms. As she listened to the words of the song, she agreed that being with him did feel so right, like nothing she'd ever felt before, in fact. But she reminded herself that she hardly knew him and had to be careful around him ... for her heart's sake.

"I'm starving," she announced when the song ended. They had stopped dancing, but kept their arms around each other. "Those shots really do drum up an appetite!"

His mouth formed a soft smile. "Food is the last thing on my mind right now."

Their eyes met and held a long moment before she forced herself away, smoothing her hair. "You're being way too French for this country girl," she said breathlessly.

"I like this country girl." He led her to the restaurant area. There, they both ordered the prime rib dinner, and Jean-Philippe chose their wine. After a glass of it, Julia was glad she was eating because she was definitely feeling the alcohol.

But she hadn't realized how much until the band began to play an old-fashioned country ballad, "Old Dogs, Children and Watermelon Wine." When Roxanne got a bit tipsy, she liked to sing the song that talked about what's really to be valued in life —like loyal old dogs who stick with you even though you make mistakes, children who are too young to know how to hate, and the simple taste of watermelon wine. Foolishly, the song, the words, brought tears to Julia's eyes. She did her best to hide them from Jean-Philippe, but to her surprise, he squeezed her hand.

"You're such a fraud, Julia Perrin," he murmured.

"What?" she asked, blinking hard.

His gaze was soft as he cupped her face then leaned forward and gently kissed her. She was stunned. "What was that for?"

"You try to act tough, but you're such a softie," he said.

She looked away. She couldn't handle him being nice to her, not when she was feeling so vulnerable.

Julia asked for a doggie bag for nearly half of her prime rib, and before it came, Jean-Philippe reached for her hand. "They're now singing yet another song about watermelons," he announced with more than a little humor in his voice. "You must show me this line dance. Come on!"

She felt as if she'd already had too much dancing and old songs tonight. "I don't think—"

"You think too much! Time to act." He helped her to her feet.

The song was "The Watermelon Crawl." Off to the side, she showed him the steps which included what Julia called "shaking the bootie." He laughed with definite appreciation when she showed him how to do it. He caught on, and they soon joined the others.

"Now, that was fun!" he said when the dancing stopped. She had to agree.

And when the slow, "It's Your Love" began, they moved together without hesitation. When the song ended, her emotions felt more twisted than ever. She had enjoyed holding him far, far too much. And she wanted him … also far too much.

"I think it's time for me to go home," she said breathlessly, reminding herself that he'd be leaving soon, that she scarcely knew him, and that she had no room for a rich, gadabout, distant cousin in her life.

After paying the bills, they left.

As they headed for Jean-Philippe's truck, they saw Deon and Shane standing on a corner in a low haze of cigarette smoke. Deon had tobacco in one hand and a flask in the other.

"Well, if it isn't the little B&B owner and her guest," Deon slurred. "I guess your women customers took off. I was expecting a call from the big one."

"They've gone," Julia said, not bothering to stop as she and Jean-Philippe passed the two men.

"Well," he grinned, "if you ever need company when *all* your guests are gone…"

"The place is all booked up," she called with finality in her voice.

He spat on the ground and they could feel his eyes watching them as they got into Jean-Philippe's truck.

"What did Crystal see in that human mold spore?" Julia muttered.

Jean-Philippe chuckled at her description. "She was merely 'looking for love in all the wrong places,'" he said, practically singing the song.

Julia couldn't help but laugh.

Jean-Philippe used his front-door key when they reached the cabin and let her in first.

Then he walked up to her, his expression serious.

The muscles in her neck and shoulders went taut, and a tightness enveloped her ribcage that made it hard to breathe as she watched him approach. Every ounce of self-preservation told her to say something cutting that would stop him in his tracks. She'd done it before with others. Why not with him? They'd had a nice evening, a great evening. In fact, it was one of the best she could remember having since … forever. And while she longed to see where it would lead to next, every nerve warned caution.

She was a ready to head upstairs.

"Julia," he whispered and held out his hand.

She stopped; her heart thrummed hard in her chest as she stared at his outstretched hand. She wasn't a child, but a woman on the downhill side of her thirties, with wants and needs. She couldn't remember ever having felt this way about a man before. It was lust, that's all. She'd known lust before, more than once—and its rather unsatisfactory conclusion. Somehow, she doubted that would be the result with Jean-Philippe.

She looked at his outstretched hand, and as much as her mind warned her to turn away, whatever it was he was offering, she wanted. She needed him. But just for tonight. And tomorrow, she would walk away and live as she always had. On her own, alone—just the way she liked it.

She took his hand, and he drew her close.

CHAPTER 18

When Julia woke up the next morning, she understood why Mallory had left a queen-sized bed in the small bedroom she had used, that Julia now used, and only put twin beds in the guest quarters. She looked at Jean-Philippe asleep beside her and studied his features so that, in the future, when he was back in France or wherever he was going next, she could remember everything about him and how it had felt to spend a magical night with him.

She was no innocent, but the few awkward boys she'd been with in college were nothing compared to a gentle, experienced, loving man who had made her feel desirable, even beautiful. She could feel his passion in his eyes and his touch. He had made no declarations of love for her, nor had she for him. Why should he? She knew he didn't love her.

She'd never been in love and wasn't even sure what it was or how it felt. And it was the last thing she wanted to feel with a man like Jean-Philippe. She couldn't even begin to imagine the beautiful women he must have had in his life—nor did she want to. So she had acted—pretended—as if their night together happened simply because they were two people, alone in the world, and happy to have found each other for a special moment.

It seemed he had believed her.

She got up, showered, dressed, and headed downstairs so she could set out breakfast and go back to being a good little B&B owner preparing a meal for her guest. But when he joined her, he attempted a kiss. She swatted him away and told him to go sit down and eat. He looked at her curiously a moment, eyebrows raised, and then did as told.

When he had some black coffee and a buttered croissant, he declared it was time for them to search for Luke's home.

They followed the road that led away from the cabin but it soon ended at an open field. No fences or "no trespassing" signs had been put up, so they entered the field and continued on.

Jean-Philippe looked around. "Where can your neighbor's house be?"

"I don't know," she admitted. "I have no idea why he walked in the direction he did, or where he ended up."

"There are no farms out here," Jean-Philippe said. "Do you know who owns this land?"

"I don't."

"This is all so unlike France," Jean-Philippe said. "Here, simple things are impossible."

"What do you mean?"

"For example, before coming to the cabin, I spent many hours searching the state archives looking for information on Elijah or Lucas Donnelly, but I found nothing. No marriage, birth, or death certificates. Nothing. I don't understand. What did they do with people who died? Just stick them in the ground where no one can find them?"

Julia hadn't thought about that before. "When the homesteads were large enough, they sometimes set aside a bit of land for a burial plot for the family, especially when out in the country where there were no churches with burial grounds." Julia paused a moment. "Come to think of it, in an area like this, most of the cemeteries were for miners. I imagine Elijah wouldn't want his wife to be buried alongside a bunch of miners. Also, since he'd bought the land and built the cabin for her. It would make sense he'd have buried her on his own land."

"You think so?" Jean-Philippe asked.

"You know, I've always wondered why there's only one acre here with the cabin. I mean, nobody had just an acre back when Elijah built his home. He should have had a minimum of ten acres, if not a lot more. Most people out in an area like this wanted a farm or a ranch. I suspect one of my ancestors sold off the land."

"Where could we find such information?"

"The County should have it. I don't know how far back the records go—but Idaho City is where everything is kept. I say we go to Idaho City and see if we can find anything about Elijah Donnelly's original stake."

"When can we go there?"

"It's barely an hour away. Let's go now."

Jean-Philippe couldn't imagine Idaho City had looked very different a hundred and fifty years earlier, except it would have been teeming with gold miners and others there to support them. In 1862 through '64, it had been the center of the biggest gold rush since the Forty-niners in California. Now, it was quiet, not quite a tourist destination, but too close to Boise and on too well-traveled a highway to become a ghost town. Some of its sidewalks were still made of wood with a roof overhang to keep snow or hot sun from the people strolling by shops, eateries, and "antique" stores.

The city had burned nearly to the ground several times over the past decades, including a major fire just recently, but the people living there loved it and kept rebuilding, much as the ones did who came before them.

"I feel like I've stepped into a Clint Eastwood Western," Jean-Philippe said.

"I've always loved Idaho City," Julia admitted.

"The more I get to know you, I can see why you would," he said with a smile and then took her hand as they walked down the street. He noticed he did that a lot, but he liked touching her —as if he was afraid she'd run off or disappear on him if he didn't. She truly reminded him of a wood nymph—a sprite— and after last night, he knew he wanted to keep her close. At least while he was here in Idaho, however long that might be. He hadn't decided yet when he would leave and had the feeling Julia's reaction to him might have a lot to do with that decision.

He couldn't read her, which was beyond frustrating. At times, he thought she liked him quite a bit, and other times, he felt he couldn't get out of her life fast enough.

But he would enjoy being here with her while it lasted. He couldn't help but inwardly cringe at that last thought. "Everyone leaves," Julia had said to him the other night. He'd wanted to deny it, but in truth, she was right.

This was an interesting interlude, but at some point he would get on with his life, with his work.

He would leave her.

In the county office building, they were directed to the assessor's office. From there, after Julia showed that she was owner of a property in Garden Valley, she was able to look at the property records.

"Oh, no." Julia's tone dripped with disgust. "Wouldn't you

know it! Roxanne was the one who sold the land. God, that woman! What didn't she ruin?" With unchecked irritation Julia read the information about her mother's losing seventy-nine acres that had surrounded the cabin because she hadn't been able to afford the taxes on it.

At least Roxanne had divided the property before she lost it. She formed one parcel consisting of the cabin and its surrounding acre, while the other seventy-nine acres bordered the river and stretched about halfway up to the Middlefork Road. It was probably because the property was land-locked, with no direct access to a road, that no one had bought it from the county.

"From what I can tell," Julia said, "Roxanne only paid taxes on the cabin's parcel. The county threatened to take the other land, and eventually, they did. Whoever buys it would have to pay all the back taxes and fees. It looks like the county put it up for auction at least twice, but both times the buyers backed out. It doesn't say why. Nothing has happened with the land for the past five years, so maybe the county forgot that they own it, or they're just waiting for someone to make an offer."

"And then someone who isn't family would own the land." He didn't like that thought one bit.

"I'm afraid so."

They got into the truck to ride back to Crouch, but then Jean-Philippe suggested they should take a circuitous route through Boise so that he could buy himself a pair of cowboy boots.

Julia looked at him as if he must be joking, but seeing it wasn't, she rolled her eyes. "Whatever."

"How strange Roxanne didn't tell you or your sisters about splitting the property," Jean-Philippe said as he drove toward Boise.

"Some years back she cut off communication with me and Carly. The only one she stayed in contact with was my Mallory. But even Mallory ended up clashing with her. None of us even heard that she had developed a heart condition, or how bad it was. Next thing we knew, she was gone."

"Such a shame that you didn't have a chance to reconcile with her," Jean-Philippe shook his head.

"It wasn't a matter of reconciling. She made her choice when she gave full custody of us to our fathers. As a child, I hated her for it. If you haven't guessed, I was a difficult kid. Even worse, I was the one who was supposed to watch my little sisters—who I scarcely knew—while she cavorted with old friends. Yet, as much as I tried to hate coming to the cabin and even tried to hate Carly and Mallory, I couldn't do it. I found that I loved being there, although I did all I could to hide it."

"It was hard for all of you, I think," Jean-Philippe murmured, looking at her as if he understood a lot more than he had before.

"Definitely."

"And your father?"

Julia almost asked, "Which one?" But she didn't. "I don't know," she said aloud.

He seemed to sense her hesitancy to reply and put his hand on her arm, giving her a light squeeze as if in support and understanding. She liked that about him, just as she liked the way his mere touch made her feel as if her whole body were on fire.

"I'm surprised that no one has offered money for your cabin yet," Jean-Philippe said after a while. "With the cabin, the rest of the property has access to the road and instantly becomes more valuable. And, it's fine land. It could be a great horse ranch. I've seen a couple of beautiful horse ranches in this area. I envy them."

"You do? You know something about horses?" she asked.

"I do." He smiled a moment, then explained. "Grandmere had a country estate outside of Paris and kept horses there. She used to say it was in her blood because her father was an American cowboy. She loved telling Parisians that. I even had my own horse, Yvette. She died at the grand age of twenty-eight, a few years ago. Grandmere gave her to me when I was eight years old and Yvette was a three-year-old filly. When she passed, I cried almost as much as when I lost Grandmere."

Julia hesitated for a moment, but then she patted his shoulder in sympathy. "I remember as a child out here seeing how attached people and their horses become to each other."

Jean-Philippe glanced at her with appreciation. "I'm glad to hear you don't find it silly."

"Not at all."

"Grandmere and I would often spend summers in the French countryside, and winters in the United States. But even in winter, I would return so I could see Yvette and let her know I hadn't forgotten her."

"That was good. But what about your mother? Didn't she care that you were away from her so much of the year?"

"She had her music, and she knew I was well cared for. Plus, Grandmere and I would often fly somewhere to see my mother perform, as well as to check on her properties. I sometimes felt as if I spent more time on a plane growing up than I did in any one house."

"A jet-setting child," she said with a smile.

"That part wasn't fun, but Grandmere and I loved summers with the horses. She rode well. I have pictures back in Paris of both of us wearing big Stetson hats and sitting on our horses.

It's rather humorous now that I see what real cowboys look like."

"I can't imagine." Julia snickered.

He grimaced teasingly. "Laugh if you wish, but those were wonderful days. I've always wanted to have my own horse ranch, but instead, I seem to still spend all my time traveling. A horse ranch, ties one down to one location. Horses need a lot of attention, but most will repay it with devotion and loyalty."

She nodded. "True, but I suspect you'd soon hate being stuck in one spot after such an adventurous childhood."

"Actually, I would love it." His tone carried a touch of wishfulness.

She was surprised to hear such a poignant admission. It made her aware, as if she needed more reminders, that she really didn't know him well at all.

"Enough about that," he said. "I wonder if, when we check out what was once your land, we might come across Elijah's family plot."

"We might."

"And let's hope it was your ghosts that stopped anyone from wanting to buy the Donnelly land and that they keep it up. It would be terrible to have the Donnelly House suddenly surrounded by a new subdivision."

"Oh, wash your mouth out with soap," Julia said with a shiver. Not until the words were out did she realize it had been one of Roxanne's favorite sayings. "All I can say is, I'm glad Roxanne at least had the sense to keep the cabin. It still amazes me that she didn't sell it. But she had a lot of secrets."

"I imagine she did," Jean-Philippe agreed. "The biggest one being why the cabin never helped her find true love."

Just then, Julia saw the street with the boot shop up ahead. She was glad not to pursue her mother's love life any further.

"We're almost there," she said, dropping the subject. "Turn right at the next light."

After Jean-Philippe bought himself a pair of handmade, black, Western-style boots that cost more than Julia made in a week at her old job, he was tempted by a pair of made-to-order Lucchese boots. But Julia-the-practical convinced him to be sure he liked wearing boots before putting out what those cost. He just smiled and went along with her suggestion.

They then went to a casual French restaurant. Jean-Philippe actually approved of the food to his surprise—and to Julia's. Finally, they returned to the cabin. Jean-Philippe was curious about Roxanne and wanted to listen to some tapes of her singing old show tunes. Julia found it impossible to refuse him such a simple request even though the songs brought with them a lot of not-so-great memories.

Still, after enough wine, Julia joined in Roxanne singing "Shall We Dance?" from *The King and I,* except that she teasingly changed the words to "Shall We Line Dance?" aiming it at Jean-Philippe.

He was both pleased and amused. "Do you know your voice is every bit as lovely as your mother's?" he asked. "You should sing all the time."

"It's not," she said, suddenly embarrassed. "And besides, there's not much to sing about."

"For you there should be," he said.

Her heart skipped a beat. But then Roxanne began to sing "If Ever I Would Leave You," from *Camelot,* one of Julia's favorite musicals. When Roxanne reached winter, wondering how she could leave him after seeing him running through the snow, the words touched too close to home. And when the words added the idea of sitting by a fire on a cold winter's evening, and Julia saw the glow from the fireplace on Jean-Philippe's handsome face, it was more than she could handle.

"That's enough for tonight," she said when the song ended. "I'm tired. I'm heading to bed."

Jean-Philippe's expression told her he, too, had been affected by the emotion in Roxanne's voice as she sang the love song. That was one thing about Roxanne, all her heart went into her singing.

"Feel free to continue to listen to songs if you wish," Julia said, standing. "Goodnight."

"Will you first, *please*, tell me what's been troubling you for days now?" he asked.

She shut her eyes a moment, then let the words fall from her lips as quickly and unemotionally as humanly possible. "Luke told me that Roxanne and Mike Halkonen were in love, that everyone thought they would marry. I believe he's my father. My real father. And I don't know what to do about it. That's all."

"Surely, you want to talk about—"

"No. Don't even try, Jean-Philippe. I don't want to hear or say anything more about it."

With that, she hurried upstairs to her bed, alone. She thought that was best. Despite their prior evening, she hadn't wanted to presume he would want to be with her again and thought she needed to return their relationship to a professional one.

But a half-hour later, when she heard a light knock on her bedroom door, she couldn't stop her pulse from racing. She opened it to Jean-Philippe. "I miss you," he whispered.

She threw her arms around him, holding him tight, and no words were needed.

CHAPTER 19

The next day, Jean-Philippe wanted to walk the property that had belonged to the Donnelly family. Julia joined him. They had the coordinates and footage from the county's map, but it was difficult to see exactly where it lay since fences had rotted years earlier, if they ever existed, and weren't all that accurate, anyway.

Jean-Philippe looked around. "If I were Elijah, and I had just lost my wife," he said, "I believe I would want her fairly close to the cabin. Not close enough that I would have to look at her grave every minute of every day, but close enough it wouldn't be too difficult to go to visit her and to take the baby with me. Also, I think I'd like her grave to be up high, so that I could imagine that, if she wanted, she could look out and see the river and the mountains beyond."

Julia agreed with what he was saying. "Up there, on that rise," she said pointing to a high piece of land not too far from the cabin.

"Let go up and see."

They could find no path. The foliage was thick, and Jean-

Philippe couldn't help but wonder, even if the area had held graves a hundred years earlier, how would they find them now?

He also wondered how Julia could remain silent about Mike Halkonen, but she'd made it quite clear to him it wasn't his business, and she wouldn't discuss it. He honored that request.

They walked up through the shrubs and he was glad for the rugged jeans and especially the boots he wore. The classic garb made even more sense with every goathead plant with razor-sharp bristles that he passed. He wondered what Grandmere would say if she saw him now. She'd probably say he was surely his great-grandfather's kin.

He also wondered what she'd think of Julia. Actually, he wondered what *he* thought of Julia. He couldn't help but think it had been a mistake to go to her room again last night. The first night they'd spent together was filled with newness and the passion of discovery. But last night … ah, last night had more depth, more heart, and—for him—it was all about wanting to be as close as possible with one very special person. He had thought she felt that way as well, but then, being Julia, although she had been warm and passionate in her bed, in the morning—as she had the morning before—she was all business, the "innkeeper," and he was her valued lodger.

He had to chuckle. That was pure Julia—the icy facade, and the passion beneath it.

None of this had been expected. She was supposed to be the strange eldest sister, living in a haunted cabin in the middle of nowhere. He never dreamed anything would happen between them, and definitely not that it would go this far.

Now, as he watched the way she carried herself as she hiked up the hillside, head high, shoulders square, back perfectly straight, watched the way the morning sun caused her pale hair to glisten, he knew this picture of her against a background of trees and brush covered with a magical layer of white hoarfrost, was something—and she was someone—he would never forget wherever life brought him.

When they had almost reached the top of the rise, he saw a small wooden structure that listed badly. Much of the wood was decayed, and the walls had missing slats. It looked like it had been a miniature chapel. Weeds seemed to be holding up the walls, and how the roof managed to stay on was anybody's guess.

"I wonder what that was," Julia said.

He had no idea. "Let's check it out."

The building's door was, amazingly, still on its hinges. But it needed to swing outward to open and weeds grew high and thick in front of it.

The two of them got on their hands and knees and used pocket knives, the only tool they had brought with them, to cut and dig up the weeds. Finally, they cleared enough ground that the door could have swung open were it not padlocked.

"The wood holding the lock is rotten," Jean-Philippe said, jiggling the door. "I think if we can get our fingers around the door and both pull on it, we'll pull off this part—what do you call it?"

"The hasp," Julia said.

"Yes, we'll pull the hasp off the wood."

She nodded. "Let's try it."

They both pulled on the door as much as they could without success. Jean-Philippe finally put his foot against the wall of the little building.

"Wait! First you must look at that cowboy boot," he said, pausing to admire his new footwear. "That's a great boot. Next, I want a real cowboy hat like they wear at Mama's. Not a big tall one, but smaller, with rolled sides and a front that dips down."

"Okay, cowboy," she said with a laugh. "Stop admiring your boots and cowboy up. In other words, get to work."

He'd have to remember that expression. "Yes, ma'am," he said with a smile and as much of a drawl as he could manage.

He then pulled on the door. Finally, the hasp broke free, and the door sprang open, causing both Julia and Jean-Philippe to land flat on their backs. They looked at each other and laughed at how silly they both felt.

"We did it," Julia said, still smiling.

It was all Jean-Philippe could do not to roll over to her and kiss her until they were both senseless as she lay there looking beautiful and completely desirable. Instead, he took a deep breath and helped her to her feet. "Now, we need to see what we've found."

He went in first, looking for snakes and vermin living inside the hut. The air was musty and smelled of wood rot and mold. But there was nothing alive inside. Not even spiders and their webs. But he saw what he'd gone inside to find.

He needed more light and pushed the door hard against the weeds to open it wider. "It's a crypt," he said softly. "And it has three headstones."

"Oh, my." Julia carefully followed him into the space.

Jean-Philippe took out his cell phone and put on the flashlight, then used his fingers and knife to carefully brush away the dirt and grime free from the first headstone.

It read:

Elijah Donnelly
Beloved Husband of Hannah and Father of Lucas
1864 - 1892

Jean-Philippe then scrubbed away the grime over the middle headstone. It was the largest and the most elaborate. It read:

Hannah Louise Donnelly

Beloved Wife of Elijah and Mother of Lucas
1868 - 1891

And last of all, a very simple stone lay over the last grave:

Lucas Truscott Donnelly
Forever in Our Hearts
1891 - 1923

Julia stood back and studied the three headstones. "This is so sad," she cried. "To think, they were here all this time but forgotten about by their family. And now, even the land they were buried on has been lost to the Donnelly clan. I feel terrible about that."

Jean-Philippe lay his arm across her shoulders and pulled her to his side, needing her warmth as he faced the cold graves. "At least we found them. To think, that's where my great-grandfather lay. And his parents, my great-great-grandparents, are here as well. It's truly hard to believe."

She leaned against him and looked up with a kind smile. "You found them, just as you promised your grandmother."

"This is all quite remarkable. More than I ever expected." He drew in his breath as he studied the graves. "But I also see now that Grandmere would have been only four years old when her father died. She always wondered if she might have been able to find him and get to know him, but now I see she was simply too young."

"It's sad he never knew what a fine daughter he had," she murmured.

"It is. Although I'll add it's also strange for me to be here after having heard about Lucas Donnelly for so many years. Grandmere had made him into an almost mythical figure—the tragic American cowboy who'd ridden off into the sunset to give the woman he loved and their child a better life. I'm glad I've found him for her."

"You did." Julia looked up at him with a warmth that did his heart good. "Somehow, I think she knows it."

He found himself touched by her words and he realized how glad he was, now that his long search had ended, that he had someone to share this moment with—someone who truly understood what it meant.

"I'm going to do all I can to buy back this land," she added. "I can't bear the thought of someone else owning our family's cemetery. Or even worse, simply plowing it up."

His eyebrows rose. "You'll buy it? How?"

"I don't know. More online gigs. Maybe I'll have to take any job in my field that opens up, experience and salaries be damned. And I'll have to advertise the cabin like crazy. Maybe even put a cot in the laundry room for me and rent out my bedroom. But I'll get the money. Whatever it takes. I don't give up."

He smiled and looked heavenward. Grandmere used to be every bit as adamant when she made a decision that seemed close to impossible. "You aren't the first woman with Donnelly blood I've heard say that."

She shrugged. "Maybe it runs in the family, but it's how I feel."

"I know. Don't worry," Jean-Philippe urged. "I, too, will make sure nothing happens to their graves."

She looked up at him. "I believe you."

The outer edges of his eyes crinkled in a smile. "You should." How could she not know how he felt about this family, this land, and most importantly, about her?

He lightly kissed her lips. It wasn't a kiss of passion, not at this gravesite setting. He meant it as a kiss of promise and much more.

She wrapped her arms around this chest and back and let her head rest on his shoulder.

That, from Julia, was all but a declaration of love. He felt about ten feet tall.

After a long moment, she let him go and said, "We need to clean up their graves. Even though this isn't my land, those are our relatives. We can't leave them like this."

Jean-Philippe nodded. "We will." The wind was picking up, and gray clouds now covered the sky. Soon, winter snows would be coming. "But before we do anything else, if Grand-mere were here, she would say a prayer for them. Let me do this for her."

He bowed his head. He glanced at her with gratitude when she took his hand and bowed her head as well as he murmured softly in French, *"Accorde-leur le repos éternel, Seigneur..."*

And, as he prayed, she joined him, whispering ever so softly in English, "Grant them eternal peace, Oh, Lord..."

CHAPTER 20

T he next morning, they saw that it had snowed overnight, and the land was dusted with white. But the sun soon came out, and although it was cold, the day was clear and bright.

Jean-Philippe went into the forest to meet with a couple of conservation officers from Fish and Game to search the area where they'd last seen the bal-chatri trap. And Julia decided to make some inquiries of her own in town.

She wished she'd been friendlier to Butch at The Rusty Nail because he seemed like the type of guy who knew a lot, maybe too much, about mostly everyone in town—which was exactly why she didn't normally talk to him.

She decided to try instead the owner of the hardware store. Fred Wilkins had been there close to forever, and she had known him as a child. As she walked into the chaotically stocked store with its narrow aisles and merchandise everywhere, he sat on the same tall stool he'd used for years. But now, his hair had turned gray, his belly looked like its own beer keg, and his glasses were coke-bottle thick. But then he smiled at her and the years melted away. She was once again the little girl in the store with a list of things to buy for her mother. Fred had always helped her figure out what it was Roxanne needed so that Julia wouldn't end up in trouble for not having gotten everything on the list.

She had loved him for that. "So good to see you again, Mr. Wilkins," she said.

"I was wondering when you'd stop by. I hear your cabin is looking real nice, and you're even using it as a bed and breakfast."

"I am. It's doing well, too."

"I know your sisters were both living there. Is it your turn now?"

"It sure is. And I like it quite a bit."

"Glad to hear it. So, what can I do you for?" he asked, using the twisted wording he was known for.

"Actually, I'm here wondering if you have any idea about a couple of guys who might be out in the forest doing something they shouldn't be."

He looked confused. "What was that?"

"It's complicated," she said with a smile. "But have you noticed anyone buying some supplies that just didn't seem to make sense for them? I know it's a very general question, and I'm not really sure what I'm asking, or if the people I'm looking for even came into town. But was there anyone who seemed maybe a little off, if you know what I mean?"

He nodded, then his round mouth scrunched up in thought. "Now that you mention it, there were a couple of guys you might say that about. Let me think. Ah, that's right—they came in here for some strong line for fishing, but nothing else. They didn't look or act like fishermen and definitely weren't your typical tourists. Besides, what they were buying wasn't right for trout fishing, and that's mostly what people try to catch up here. Made no sense."

She thought about the many loops on the wire cage that were used to trap the falcon's talons—loops that were translucent. "Fishing line is kind of transparent, isn't it?"

"I take it you aren't a fisherman." Fred grinned. "Yes, it's as transparent as possible."

"Do you remember what those guys looked like?"

"Well, let's see. Takes a while, old brain cells, you know. But it's coming back to me. In fact, they were in here more than once. That's right! The second time was even stranger. They wanted to buy squirrel food and little cages, like you'd put hamsters in. I told them they needed a pet store for that. It was weird. They didn't seem like the type that liked small, furry critters."

"Little cages." She shuddered thinking about what falcons ate.

"Anyway, all I can tell you is the big one was broad shouldered, with a deep-tan and brown hair. His voice boomed and that man never stopped flapping his lips. I swear, I don't know how he had time to breathe. The little one was more pale, colorless. His dark hair was kind of stringy, and he looked constantly scared of the big fellow. The most he ever did was nod or mumble 'uh, huh.'"

Oh, my God. Her breathing quickened, but she wasn't all that surprised. Even Nathan had made it clear there was something he didn't like about those guys. "Do you remember if you ever heard the names Deon or Shane?" she asked.

"No, can't say that I did."

"Did they use credit cards?"

"I don't know anyone who'd be fool enough to take a card or a check from the likes of those two. Strictly cash."

She gathered a few things to buy and then was on her way. "You've been really helpful, Mr. Wilkins. Thanks so much." "Good to see you, Julia. Be careful out there all by yourself." She smiled. She'd forgotten how much she'd always like him. "I will," she promised. "Oh, I just thought of something else. I'm wondering if you know a family that lives out in my area. The son's name is Luke. I'd say he's in his early thirties. His parents are elderly and they live on a farm. I don't know their last name."

He looked puzzled. "Can't say as I can think of anyone like that," he said. "Although they sound like the type of people I should know.

He was right, she thought. "Okay. Thanks."

When she got back to the cabin, she only had to wait a little while before Jean-Philippe returned. His mouth was a grimace. "No sign at all of the smugglers. Of course, the snow didn't help. But we're afraid they may have moved to completely different locations."

She could hear the anger and frustration in his voice. "Oh, no. I'm so sorry."

"The question is where? It'll be harder than ever to find out who they are."

"I've got some information that might help." She told him about her conversation with Fred Wilkins.

"I don't believe it!" Jean-Philippe ran his hands through his hair and paced, looking at her as if she were either Einstein or Svengali. "I mean, I do believe it's those two guys, but I don't believe how easily you managed to find it out. That's great. Can I use the landline to call it in? It'll give the police something to do to try to trace them. Did you ever hear their last names?"

"The only one I remember is Deon Simms because Crystal wouldn't stop talking about how great he is. Talk about bad taste in men!"

Jean-Philippe nodded. "I'm sure he's the leader. I can't imagine him ever taking orders from Shane."

Julia smiled. "Me neither."

After he made the call, Julia told him she was going to drive back to Cascade because her print job was ready to be picked up. Ever since getting the call, the idea of facing Mike Halkonen again had preyed on her mind and she decided she needed to get it over with.

"Would you like me to go with you?" Jean-Philippe asked.

"No need," she said.

"Let's put it this way." He walked up to her and stood directly in front of her. "Would you object to me going with you?"

She didn't know how she was going to handle facing Mike Halkonen. Having Jean-Philippe there only made the situation more awkward. Of course, she could just go in, get her materials, pay him, and leave.

"Okay," she said, resigned. "You can come."

CHAPTER 21

Julia walked into the print shop, her heart pounding as she struggled to appear calm.

Mike Halkonen bent over a small table with a pencil and paper. He looked up and his eyes widened, but then he quickly turned away and moved her print jobs from a shelf to the counter. He handed her a business card and the brochure. "You might want to take a look and make sure they're what you want." His voice sounded brisk and harsh.

She took the items from him and looked them over, then handed them to Jean-Philippe. "What do you think?"

He moved closer and studied the materials. "They look great."

Julia faced Halkonen. "We'll take them."

He got a box and began moving the materials into it. As she watched him silently work, still not looking at her, she wanted to say something. But what? She stood there, staring at him.

He put the lid on the box. "Credit card?"

"Oh. Yes." She took out her wallet and found the card for him. Her hand shook as she turned it over.

He swiped it, and in a moment was handing her the receipt to sign. She looked at him, about to speak, but then saw a pen on the counter. "Excuse me," she said as she reached for it.

"Sure. Sorry."

She ran her tongue over her bottom lip. It felt dryer than the Sahara. Heart thumping, she signed the paper and handed it back.

"Thanks." He pushed the box toward her.

She picked it up, gazed a long, silent moment at Halkonen, then turned to leave.

"Stop," Jean-Philippe said.

Julia froze, hugging the box of printed materials tighter. Halkonen looked questioningly at him.

Jean-Philippe faced the shopkeeper. "She knows who you are."

Halkonen's face lost its color. "I don't know what you mean," he muttered as he concentrating on putting the cap back on the pen Julia had used.

"She knows about you and Roxanne Donnelly."

Julia stepped closer to him. "Jean-Philippe, please," she whispered.

Halkonen snorted, his eyes hard as he stared at Jean-Philippe. "So, there are still gossips around Crouch. What else is new?" He still refused to meet Julia's eyes.

"It's more than gossip," Jean-Philippe added. "As anyone can tell who looks at the two of you."

"Our looks are hardly unique." Halkonen turned his back on them and scribbled something on a tablet, then glanced over his shoulder. "You two should go up to Roseberry about fifteen miles north. That's where a lot of Finns settled years ago— including my family. There's nothing special about me."

"But how many of them were in love with Roxanne Donnelly?" Jean-Philippe demanded.

Julia grabbed his arm. "Let's go, please."

"No." He turned to Halkonen. "I've watched your daughter eating her heart out ever since she learned about you and Roxanne. And now, she's here, and you don't have the decency to even look at her. What kind of man are you?"

Halkonen's eyes were hard, and his cheeks had become mottled red. "You think this is easy for me? I wish I'd never met Roxanne Donnelly. She destroyed my life!"

Julia couldn't remain silent. "What do you mean?"

Finally, he glanced at her, a quick, angry look, and then he bowed his head. "It goes back years, to high school. We were just kids. I was the new guy in school, and most were terrible to me. Roxanne was the only one who wasn't. That's all there was to it." He raised his eyes to hers. "Who told you about us?"

"I doubt you know him."

"Who?" His voice was harsh.

"His name is Luke."

His mouth dropped. "Luke?" He spat out the word. "You mean one of the cabin's ghosts? Roxanne used to talk about him, too. She even claimed she saw him a couple of times."

Julia was shocked to hear such words. "He's not a ghost!"

Halkonen pounded his fist on his counter. "You know exactly what he is. You're every bit as crazy as your mother was."

Julia stepped back in shocked silence.

Jean-Philippe put his arm around her. "You have no right to talk to her that way."

"It's my shop," Halkonen said, his voice calmer now. "I want you both out of here."

Jean-Philippe didn't move, and his grip tightened on Julia. "How long have you run this shop?"

Halkonen looked surprised by the question, but his jaw tightened. "Seventeen years. What's it to you?"

"A bit before your son was born—around the time you got married, I imagine?"

"How would you know when I married?" Halkonen growled.

"Because that's when Roxanne stopped coming to Garden Valley." Jean-Philippe let Julia go and stepped closer to Halkonen. "When she stopped bringing her daughters here; when she stopped seeing you. Which means you knew about Julia all those years and did nothing. How could you ignore that she was your daughter?"

Halkonen's jaw worked as if he were grinding his teeth, then his eyes darted back and forth from Julia to Jean-Philippe. "What was I supposed to do?" he asked, his voice raspy, broken. "Roxanne told me the girl was Hugh Perrin's child. That was why they married so soon. And that was why she gave him custody of the girl when the two divorced."

He shut his eyes and shook his head. "I suspected otherwise, but that was Roxanne. Always telling tales, always wanting something better than what she had, including me, the short, scrawny guy from high school that she loved with all her heart, even though she wouldn't admit it. But it was me she came looking for each summer. I lived for those days. I moved up here to Cascade so no one in Garden Valley would know. I did it all because I knew how she felt, even though she tried to deny it. Nothing she did mattered. I loved her, all right? For years. Too many years, going along with whatever she said, whatever she wanted. Going along with her lies."

Julia believed every word he said. She knew the kind of loyalty and love people—men—felt for Roxanne, and how Roxanne never appreciated any of them. Not her husbands, or her daughters, and obviously, not the one man she might have really loved. Her heart ached to hear her father's pain.

Halkonen's eyes shifted from Jean-Philippe to Julia a couple of time before he sucked in air through his teeth. "When we were young she was so kind, so beautiful, and with talent to spare. But then ambition gripped her and as the years went by, she seemed to grow more bitter and spiteful. Until I said enough. I couldn't take it anymore."

"Why?" Julia whispered the word. "What made her that a way?"

He looked at her a long time, then shut his eyes. Not until he opened them again did he answer. "Disappointment, I suspect. With her career. The men in her life. Me. And I think, most of all, with herself. But I don't really know. Eventually, I managed not to care. So, are you happy now?"

Julia couldn't speak in the face of such anguish.

"Why won't you at least acknowledge your daughter?" Jean-Philippe asked, also clearly moved by Halkonen's words. "Are you so afraid of your wife's reaction?"

"I'm divorced." Halkonen's face filled with a sad bitterness painful to see. "The marriage never stood a chance. It was as the ghosts said, if you don't go along with the person they find for you, you'll never find happiness in love or anything else. Look at me. I'm proof that everything said about them is true. And so was Roxanne. All I want now is to be left alone."

"Your daughter is a good person, Mr. Halkonen," Jean-Philippe said. "Someone you should be proud of."

Halkonen dropped his gaze and said nothing. After a while, Jean-Philippe led Julia from the store.

As Jean-Philippe drove Julia back to the cabin, Halkonen's words played over and over in her mind. He obviously didn't want her interrupting his life. She could understand that, just as she could understand his bitterness. Roxanne had lied to him, although he had loved her for years. She wondered if the time

Halkonen saw her outside the ice cream parlor was when he first realized the full extent of Roxanne's lies, or if he already knew and it hadn't mattered to him.

She would never know. Nor, frankly, did she want to.

"At least it's all much clearer to me now," Julia said, trying but failing to keep the bitterness from her voice even as her eyes filled with tears. "And I owe Hugh Perrin an apology. I wondered why he never seemed to care. If he knew about Mike Halkonen and Roxanne, he would have seen my resemblance to Roxanne's old boyfriend. People always commented how I didn't look like my father. But I ignored them. Obviously, he was my dad. How could he not be?" She leaned back against the headrest and angrily wiped away the tears that fell.

"You are who you are, and that's a fine woman," Jean-Philippe said. "I can't help but suspect that someday, maybe a month from now, maybe a year, but someday, Mike Halkonen will show up at your door and say he wants to get to know his daughter. He seems like a good man who was deeply hurt on many levels and is still bitter about it. You showing up was a reminder to him of all that happened years ago. And keep in mind that while we see your resemblance to him, I'm sure he sees your resemblance to Roxanne, the woman he loved beyond reason, and who ruined his chance for a happy life. You're a reminder of all that. The love and the heartbreak."

"I don't know that I want to get to know him," Julia said. "He wants nothing to do with me. Why should that change?"

Jean-Philippe stopped the truck along the side of the road and pulled Julia to his chest. To her surprise, she found her arms going around him, holding him tight as more tears fell. "It'll be all right," he whispered. "You two are both hurting right now, but trust me, he'll come around, and I've gotten to know you well enough to know that you will, as well."

"He sounded like he hates me."

"No, he doesn't. He hates what you remind him of—he hates all that he lost." Jean-Philippe ran his thumb over her cheek to brush away some tears, then lifted her chin so her eyes met his. "Remember how he looked at his son? How he talked about him now being able to drive? He's a proud father. And in time he's going to realize he has more than one child to be proud of. I'm sure in his mind, he tried to dismiss you as much as he did Roxanne. But meeting you, now, he should know you're as different from your mother as possible. Believe me, Julia. He'll find you. Trust me on that. And in time, you'll come to like each other—probably more than either of you, right now, could ever imagine."

She sat up straight and nodded. "Thank you. Maybe you're right. Maybe ... I hope."

"Here." He handed her some napkins he's stuffed in the truck's door pockets from the last time he'd stopped at McDonald's. "Wipe your eyes and nose. You're a mess."

That made her laugh a little, but she did as told, and he again began the drive south to Garden Valley. But she couldn't stop thinking of how, if he hadn't been there, if he hadn't realized exactly all that was going on and hadn't spoken up, she would still be in limbo about Mike Halkonen and what had happened between him and Roxanne.

It was actually gutsy of Jean-Philippe to insert himself like that. It could have gone very wrong—not that it went well—but it might have been a lot worse. She understood, though, that he had done it for her.

And she ... liked him for that. Liked him a whole lot. She couldn't remember anyone else ever standing up for her that way.

She was facing away from Jean-Philippe as she thought those things, looking out at the passing scenery ...

"Pull over!" Julia cried out suddenly, grabbing the dashboard, and swiveling around to look back as they passed a gas station/food mart/restaurant complex near Smith's Ferry.

"What?" Jean-Philippe asked.

"A truck. Outside that restaurant. It looks like Deon's."

Jean-Philippe made a U-turn and soon pulled into the gas station. He slowly drove by the cars parked in front of the restaurant. Julia wrote down the green F-150's license number as they went by.

"It does look like their truck," Jean-Philippe said. "But I'm not sure it is. Are you?"

"No. I can go into the food mart, buy something, and look for them."

"It's too dangerous. Men like that are paranoid. You don't want to make them suspicious."

"I'll be careful."

"We wait right here." His words were firm. "We have the license number. If Deon and Shane come out and get into the truck, I'll use the satellite phone to call my Fish and Game contact. He'll get word to the Idaho State Police, and they'll pick those guys up. We just need to know if they head north or south on the highway."

She agreed it made sense.

Twenty minutes later, Deon and Shane walked out of the restaurant. "It's them," Jean-Philippe said as the two got into the truck and drove south, toward Boise.

Jean-Philippe called the conservation officer. "Drive," Julia told him. "Tell the officer I'll give him the information. Those guys might turn off the highway somewhere. They might just have moved their smuggling camp out here. We won't know that if we lose them."

Jean-Philippe agreed and handed her the phone while he headed south.

Julia gave the officer the make of the truck, the license, and descriptions of Deon and Shane, then hung up. The truck was still ahead of them. Jean-Philippe stayed back as far as he dared. He and Julia had recognized Deon's truck, and Deon could very likely recognize theirs as well.

"I hope the ISP shows up soon," Jean-Philippe said.

"Me, too," Julia said. "We can't let that truck out of our sight."

Jean-Philippe did his best to stay far enough behind so Dean and Shane wouldn't realize they were being followed, but also to keep them in sight. A long straight stretch made that difficult, and he slowed down considerably, but when he reached a curve in the roadway, the F-150 was no longer to be seen.

Jean-Philippe sped up to see if they had simply gotten a lot farther along the road than he'd expected, but Deon's truck appeared to have left the highway. They then reversed course, looking for side roads that the truck might have turned off on, but if it had, it was long gone.

He called his contact to give information on the area where they'd lost sight of Deon's truck.

They then continued to Crouch.

Once in Crouch, Julia asked Jean-Philippe to stop at shops up and down the Middlefork Road and the small town square area so she could leave copies of the new Donnelly House brochure with them. "Are you sure you feel up to doing that?" he asked. "After the scene with your father, you had an emotional morning."

"I know, but I'd rather do that than go back to the cabin and stew about it."

He nodded. He understood. Somehow, she knew he would.

As they visited the shops, she was amazed at how welcoming

the people she met were. They all wished her luck with her business.

One of the places on their route was the McDermott Auto Repair owned by Julia's new brother-in-law.

"Hey, there," Gunnar said, welcoming them both.

Julia explained about the brochure and handed him several for customers who might need a room for the night. He was impressed.

"Julia tells me your parents own a farm in the area," Jean-Philippe said.

"Yes. Alfalfa mainly, plus some vegetables."

"Alfalfa? So do you, by chance, work with horse ranches and stables?" Jean-Philippe asked.

"We do."

"I'm interested in possibly starting a horse ranch. I've got my eye on a nearby piece of property"—he glanced at Julia—"that would be perfect for it. I was involved with one in France, and unless things are very different here, I have the experience. We should talk sometime soon, if you have time."

Julia gawked at Jean-Philippe. She hadn't thought he was really serious about wanting to stay in Garden Valley on Donnelly land. She thought he was just musing about a possible future, not one he planned to actively pursue. And how would she fit in?

The thought was … was what? Scary. Yes, but something more. Nice? Incredible? Impossible-to-believe-yet-he'd-said it?

Jean-Philippe noticed the way Julia was staring at him, and turned to her, his eyebrows high and a smile on his face.

Gunnar looked from one to the other, curious as to what was going on. "Sure," he said. "Anytime. Give me a call."

"I will. *Merci.*"

"By the way," Julia said with a shake of the head as she tried to put aside Jean-Philippe's horse ranch idea … for the moment.

She faced Gunnar, remembering his work with veterans, "do you know a fellow, former military, who lives out near the cabin and is named Luke or Lucas? He has bad lungs—maybe from a gas attack—in the Middle East. I think he's a little older than you and lives with his parents on a farm."

Gunnar thought a moment, but then shook his head. "I'm sorry. I can't recall anyone like that."

"Thanks," Julia said. "We should get going."

Gunnar nodded. "Oh, by the way, Mal and I are in a nice little rental house, but Christmas is coming soon, and she's going to decorate it, and I know she wants to do a big dinner. Maybe you two can join us. That is, if you're still here, JP?"

Jean-Philippe glanced at Julia who stood mute and expressionless, then faced Gunnar. "Well, if I'm still here, I would like to join you very much."

"I'll be here," Julia said, forcing a stiff smile. "Tell my little sis I'll gladly attend. And it had better be good."

Gunnar grinned. "That's the Jules I know. Will do."

Julia and Jean-Philippe soon left.

Before returning to the cabin, the two stopped at The Rusty Nail for a dinner of burgers.

"I don't think you've met Julia Perrin," Jean-Philippe said to Butch as they stopped at the bar for beers before sitting down for dinner. "Julia, this is Butch."

"Nice to meet you," Julia said, holding out her hand.

Butch's wiry eyebrows were somewhere up around his hairline as his eyes jumped between Jean-Philippe and Julia. He shook her hand. "Glad to meet you, too. I know your sisters. I understand you're the one running the bed and breakfast now."

"In fact," Julia said, "here are a few brochures. If someone comes in looking for a place, I might be able to help."

"Thanks. I'll keep them near the cash register," Butch said, then poured their beers.

"So, you're enjoying it here, I take it," Butch said to Jean-Philippe as he put the beers in front of them, then cocked his head slightly in Julia's direction.

"Very much," Jean-Philippe said with a smile. "I'm thinking I might be here a lot longer than I'd planned."

Butch looked from one to the other. "Sounds good."

"Say," Julia said. "Did you happen to know a man named Mike Halkonen? He lived here some years ago."

Butch nodded. "Mike ... yeah, sure I know him. Boy, haven't seen him for years. He was a really nice guy. About my age. His folks moved into town when he was in high school, but being a stranger and not exactly 'captain of the football team' material he wasn't treated all that well. You know how teenagers can be. In fact the one who was the nicest to him was ..." He stopped then, his eyes wide as he looked at Julia. His eyebrows rose, but almost as quickly he shook his head as if dismissing the thought. "Well, anyway, like I said, he moved away. Why are you asking?"

"Nothing." Julia said with a small smile. "I just happened to hear his name. I was curious. Nothing more."

Butch nodded. "Well, your waitress is indicating your table is ready."

They thanked Butch and headed for the table, taking their beer with them.

CHAPTER 22

J ulia woke up abruptly. She lay in bed, eyes open. All was silent, but she couldn't get over the impression that she'd heard glass breaking. She rolled over, smoothed out her pillow, shut her eyes, and immediately opened them again. She felt in her bones that something was wrong.

Throwing on a robe, she tiptoed out to the hallway. She heard a scratching sound downstairs.

After drawing a deep breath, she quietly stepped into Jean-Philippe's room. Last night, she'd been so upset about Miika Halkonen, she told Jean-Philippe she needed time alone, which he'd given her. Now, she was surprised to see Pumpkin curled at the foot of his bed. She'd wondered where the little cat slept. She shook his shoulder. He opened his eyes as she put one finger over her mouth in a shushing sign. He immediately took in her worry as well as her sign to stay quiet. "What?" he mouthed.

She gestured for him to join her. He was wearing pajama bottoms as he slid out of bed and went to his door. He, too, heard the scratching, shuffling sounds.

"Do you have a firearm in the house?" he whispered.

She shook her head. "Nothing. I never dreamed…"

"A baseball bat? Anything strong?"

"Not up here. I'm sorry!"

He put on a sweatshirt and shoes. "I'm going downstairs."

"No, it's too dangerous."

"It's probably kids," he said. "They'll run as soon as they know someone is awake."

She thought of the smugglers and took hold of his arm. "What if it isn't?"

"There's one way to find out. If it's kids, they run. If not, lock the bedroom door."

She gave him a quick hug, then let him go but followed as he eased his way to the switch that controlled the lights over the stairs and turned them on.

"So you're here," Deon said as he left the great room and stood in the foyer looking up at them. In his hand was a gun.

"Run!" Jean-Philippe said to Julia.

She ducked into the bedroom, expecting him to come with her. But he stood there, as if ready to take on Deon alone … and unarmed.

"Just leave," he said to Deon.

Deon walked to the stairs and put one foot on the bottom step. "Yeah, well you deciding to play the big shot and confront us sort of ruined that idea now, didn't it?"

"You don't want to get into any more trouble than you're already in because of the falcons."

Deon smugly cocked his head. "I'm not in any trouble without proof. And soon, you'll have none."

"Proof of breaking and entering is pretty clear to me," Jean-Philippe said, arms folded and his stance defiant. "Fish and Game has your name and license. You won't get far."

Deon pointed the gun at him. "Us breaking in here is the least of your problems, Frenchie. You and your little tart."

"Come on, Deon," Shane said, now hovering near the front door. "This is going too far. You said we were just going to grab any evidence and leave."

"It's too late for that," Deon roared. "We get rid of him!"

"Please, Deon," Shane wailed.

"Listen to your friend," Jean-Philippe said.

"You'll have to get rid of me, too," Julia said, stepping beside Jean-Philippe. "Or, you can go. Rip out the landline if you don't trust us. You'll have a good start before we can reach anyone to call for help."

"Listen to her, Deon," Shane cried. "Let's get out of here!"

"Shane," Julia said. "How can you do this? I saw you with Nan. You seemed to like her."

"Shut up, all of you!" Deon said, then his eyes hard. "Shane, go outside. Get in the truck."

Shane looked up at Julia, but then hung his head and did as Deon said, leaving the front door open.

Deon took a step up, then another, as Jean-Philippe backed toward the bedroom, his arm extended to keep Julia behind him. "Stop!" Deon ordered. He looked as if he was about to run up the stairs when his legs suddenly flew up and out from under him. He landed face first, with his chin smacking hard against a step. He then slid, thumping his way down the staircase like a slinky toy, to the foyer. His gun dropped from his hand.

Jean-Philippe started down to pick it up, but Deon somehow managed to crawl to the gun before Jean-Philippe could reach it. Jean-Philippe froze and began to slowly go back up the stairs.

Dazed, Deon was attempting to stand up when the long carpet runner that stretched over the foyer from the front door to the great room suddenly jerked out from under his feet. He somersaulted in mid-air, once more dropping the gun, and came down on his head, out cold.

Jean-Philippe again started down the stairs, but then stopped and stared as Deon began to roll across the floor, the hall runner circling his body as he went, much like wrapping thread around a spool, trapping him inside it.

Jean-Philippe picked up the gun. "Julia! Come down and phone the police. I have no idea how it happened, but we just caught Deon."

She came down in time to see the truck's headlights as Shane backed out of the driveway and peeled down the road.

———

The Sheriff's deputies left with Deon in handcuffs, and word had already come that Shane had been stopped before he made it out of Crouch. By mutual, albeit unspoken, consent, Julia and Jean-Philippe didn't talk about the magic carpet antics they had witnessed while the sheriff and his men were there.

Now, relieved, they walked into the great room to see what damage had been done. Shattered glass on a French door pane near the lock showed how Deon and Shane had entered the cabin. They saw their laptops stacked on the coffee table and guessed the two men had planned to take them. Elijah Donnelly's portrait had been removed from the mantle, and furniture that had been against the walls was now pulled away.

"What were they looking for?" Julia wondered aloud.

"Probably cameras and other birder equipment," Jean-Philippe said. "All of which I keep out in the truck, which might not be the safest place for it." He went out to his truck and came back in with a smile and his backpack. "Luckily, they didn't think I'd be dumb enough to leave it out there. They were wrong!"

She smiled at the way he put himself down. He was anything but dumb. "You're too trusting sometimes."

"Maybe." Then he waggled his eyebrows. "Or more clever than even I realize."

"I'll clean up this glass," she said. "Maybe you can look for wood or a cardboard to cover the hole in the French door window so we don't freeze in here before we can fix it."

As she swept up the glass he walked around looking for something to cover the hole. "What's this?" he asked. Along the wall where the credenza had stood, he found a small section of log that looked loose.

She put down the broom and went over to where he was kneeling. "I've never noticed that before."

He wriggled the log. "It can come out. Shall I pull on it?"

"Why not?"

He did and found a hidden compartment built in the wall. Inside was a small, flat wooden box. He handed it to Julia.

It had a metal clasp but no lock. With a twist of the clasp, she lifted the lid. Inside were a couple of old papers, stiff and brown with age, and two equally old envelopes. She unfolded the top paper.

"Oh, my goodness. This is Elijah and Hannah's marriage certificate. This box must have been theirs. I can't imagine how it remained hidden in that cubby hole all these years. Not with all the renovations done here."

Jean-Philippe looked at her and gave a slight shake of the head. "We just watched a carpet wrap itself around a man like he was the stuffing in a crêpe, and you're going to wonder why we're the only ones who ever noticed a loose piece of log? I can't help but suspect we did not find this by chance."

She glanced at Elijah's portrait, still leaning against the wall. He looked happy. "Point taken."

Jean-Philippe also looked up at Elijah. "Good job, old man."

The portrait suddenly seemed to be frowning, but Julia couldn't remember seeing anything actually move on it.

With a shake of her head, she then turned to the certificate. "It says that Hannah Louise Truscott, age twenty-two of Philadelphia, Pennsylvania, married Elijah Donnelly, age twenty-six, of Idaho City, Idaho, on June 21, 1890, in Chicago, Illinois. How interesting that they married there. I wonder why."

"I suspect the answer is in the box," Jean-Philippe said.

Next, she took out a letter, undated. She read it aloud:

My dearest Elijah,

I have no idea what do to. Madison brought home a friend of his, an attorney in his law firm named Peter Herring—like the fish. He's some sort of mentor to Madison, and unmarried. My father and Madison made it clear that I'm supposed to become Peter's wife. Not only is his name a fish—he reminds me of one. I hate him, Elijah! I don't know what to do. I can't stay here. I can't marry him.

Dare I confess to you that I thank God every day that you visited this city last year and destiny allowed us not only to meet, but to feel an immediate bond. I believe that bond has grown and become ever stronger through our correspondence these past months.

I know I should not be so forward, but there's only one person I would ever want to marry. I hope you know who I mean.

You've never given any hint that your thoughts might go in such a direction. As for me, our summer together was the most wonderful time of my life. And so, my dearest Elijah, if you never want to have anything more to do with such a wanton woman as I, then I understand.

But know that you shall remain forever in my heart,
Hannah

. . .

"I like her," Julia said. "She wasn't afraid to let him know how she felt, which, I imagine was very difficult to do back then."

She then found a small envelope and inside were train ticket stubs, all from June 1890. One was from Philadelphia to Chicago, and then Chicago to Boise. Another was a round trip from Boise to Chicago and back. "I'm sure these tickets mean they eloped," Julia said. She smiled as she held the stubs in her hand, almost as if she could feel the excitement and joy of the two lovers. "They met in Chicago, got married, and then travel together to Idaho. Good for them!"

There was only one thing left in the box, an envelope with the name "Thomas Donnelly" on it. The envelope had not been sealed, and it had no address or indication it was ever sent.

"I believe Thomas may have been Elijah's brother," Julia said, taking a folded letter from the envelope.

"I doubt he'd care that you read his letter," Jean-Philippe said. "Especially since Elijah never sent it, but he felt it was important enough that he put it in here and hid it away."

She nodded and opened the letter, then read,

Dear Thomas,

I'm sorry I've been so remiss in contacting you. The cabin is finished now, and we are relieved to be living in it at last. I hope this finds you and Mary and your sweet Sarah and Theodore well.

Now, for my good news. You are to become an uncle! Hannah is with child. We are overjoyed. It is my hope that, finally, Hannah will feel at home here.

In truth, things have been difficult for her. I hesitate to burden you with my problems, but I am forced to wonder if, at times, Hannah doesn't regret her decision to become my wife. Life on our farm is hard, and she is so delicate, it worries me. She doesn't complain, but I can see the weariness in her face, and the skin beneath her eyes has a perma-

nent purple hue of fatigue. I often think I never should have allowed her to come here.

Perhaps I should have pretended not to love her so that she would still be safe and warm and living a life of luxury with her servants back in Philadelphia. Instead, she followed me here because her heart is so big and she had more love than common sense. Maybe I do as well. If I had been thinking, I would have gone to live with her in Philadelphia and not brought her out to this rough, desolate land.

I worry about her constantly. I know she loves me, but sometimes I wonder if it's enough for

"It's unfinished," Julia said. "I can understand why he hesitated to send it, hesitated to burden his brother with all this. Poor man."

Jean-Philippe's sad eyes met Julia's. "If he already felt so much guilt about bringing Hannah to live in an area she was ill-equipped for, I can't imagine how he felt when she died in childbirth."

Julia gazed at the picture of Elijah. "I'm so sorry," she said to him. "So sorry that you had to bear such grief."

CHAPTER 23

The next day, Jean-Philippe and Julia met with the Fish and Game chief as well as the Idaho State Police to give statements about Deon and Shane.

Apparently, as soon as Shane was arrested, he had folded and tried to put all the blame on Deon, even showing the State Police where they were keeping the eight peregrine falcons they had captured. Shane's biggest sorrow was that they hadn't managed to capture a gyrfalcon. As "nice" as Shane had seemed compared to Deon, he was more than a little crazy and liked capturing falcons to stop them from eating the small birds he not only loved, but seemed to identify with.

It turned out that Deon had needed Shane's help because he didn't understand computers well at all. As a result, Shane's computer had been used to work with the bigwigs behind the smuggling operation, and since Shane saved everything, his computer files offered a lot of information for the U.S. Fish and Wildlife Service. They were ecstatic by the find.

Jean-Philippe and Julia left after being given many thanks and kudos for the work they did.

"I guess Shane doesn't know," Jean-Philippe said as he and Julia walked to his truck, "that Deon was going to sell the falcons to people who use them to capture smaller birds purely for sport, whereas falcons in the wild only capture what they need to in order to stay alive."

"It's sad," Julia said, "the harm men can do even when they think they're actually doing something good."

"At least we stopped a group of smugglers. We make a good team, Jules," he said, emphasizing the family pet name he'd heard used.

"Yes, we do, cowboy," she said with a big grin as they climbed into the truck to ride back to the cabin.

That afternoon, Julia and Jean-Philippe decided to walk the perimeter of what had once been Donnelly land. Holding the topographical map he'd gotten from the county, Jean-Philippe was able to determine with some accuracy the area that the county now owned.

"Were you serious about what you said to Gunnar?" Julia asked as they walked. "That you're thinking about creating your own horse ranch?"

"I am." He stopped and looked out over the surrounding area. Much of it was flat grassland, but there were areas with firs and cottonwoods, and the rise where they'd found the graves. "This land would be perfect. Rolling pastures, plenty of water. I could see building a barn, stables, and paddocks not far from the house."

"You want to buy the Donnelly land?" she asked.

He faced her, his expression serious. "Is it so crazy for me to want to stay here?"

She froze. "But you would also need the cabin's land for access."

"I know." He drew in his breath. "Do you think …? Can you see yourself …?"

She shook her head and walked away, turning her back on him and facing the river. After a while she said, "You've talked about traveling all over the world. Of your … wealth. I assume you're talking about some sort of partnership. But, frankly, I don't see you being content, let alone happy, staying in a place like this for very long. And once you leave, what would happen to it? Who would care for the horses?"

He took her arms and made her face him. "I've traveled a lot, yes. And you know what? Through all those travels I was looking for a place I wanted to stay. To *stay*, Julia. To put down roots, to have a place I cared about, that I looked forward to returning to as often as possible—someplace, I should say, that wasn't the stable where my horse, Yvette, lived," he added with a quick smile. "But that's the one thing I never had, one thing my family's money couldn't buy. Maybe that was why I was so happy to take on Grandmere's search. Somehow, deep down, I knew I was searching for much more than a grave. And here, I believe I've found it."

She stepped away from him and his arms dropped.

"We must be practical. You haven't been here long at all," she said.

He stepped to her side, his hands in his pockets. "You'd be surprised how fast a person can become attached to a place—and a person—that they hope will become a part of their life."

She shook her head. "Jean-Philippe—"

He put a finger over her lips, stopping her. "You don't have to say it." A brief silence followed. "I see, now, that you don't feel the way I do. Maybe all I can hope for is that you will find room for me in your life as a friend."

Her heart sank. How could she make him understand? "That's not it at all," she said. "The problem is that I don't *belong* in your life! When I think of the elegant women your grandmother introduced you to, and then I look at myself. I ... I feel ridiculous." She rubbed her forehead, knowing that somehow she needed to make him understand. "I'm not a part of your world, Jean-Philippe. We both know that."

His mouth tightened as he met her gaze. "Do you see any of those women with me? I don't." He shook his head. "Julia, I wish you could see yourself as I see you. Yes, you're tough and outdoorsy, but at the same time you're warm and loving and both comfortable yet exciting to be around."

"But I'm not—"

"It took me a long time to understand why I couldn't decide between Greenland or Spain. Or Outer Mongolia or Timbuktu, for all that it matters. It's because I don't want to leave here. I don't want to leave you."

She shook her head. "Your words are nice, but..."

"Stop, please," he said. "I recognize that you've had a harsh burden to carry. You've learned to distrust people and to run in the opposite direction when anyone tries to get close to you. But you can't let what your parents did to you control the rest of your life. You deserve more than that. *I'm not them.* And I'm not *like* them."

She ached down to her bones as she listened to his words. She wanted so much to believe him, to tell him how she felt, but a lifetime of distrust and caution wasn't easy to toss aside. Excruciating seconds ticked by.

"I..." He drew in his breath. "I'm afraid I've fallen in love with you. I know you aren't ready to hear any such proclamations from me. But I want you to know how I feel."

She dropped her gaze for a long moment before meeting his eyes. "I believe you mean that now, but..."

His shoulders slumped. "I see." Then, he tightened his lips and gave a quick nod. "Well, if you can't trust me, there's no way I can expect you to love me." He paused a moment, but then his face grew firm, his eyes empty. "Let me know if it's okay for me to buy the Donnelly acres. I'll give them to you and your sisters. I'd hate to think some developer might buy them to put in a bunch of houses. Please give my regrets about Christmas to Mallory and Gunnar."

She stared at him, unable to speak.

He waited a moment, then walked away.

CHAPTER 24

Julia watched Jean-Philippe walk up to the rise, up to his family's graves.

She'd done it. She'd finally managed to hurt him enough that he gave up. She should be glad.

He had told her he loved her and she had told him she didn't believe him. Good job, Julia!

She headed toward the river. She needed to think, to be alone. When she was young, especially while in high school and even for a while in college, even *she* used to hope that someday a magnificent Prince Charming would show up at her door, glass slipper in hand, and promise to whisk her away from her miserable life and love her forever.

She shut her eyes a moment. Jean-Philippe fit that bill better than she could ever have imagined possible.

But instead of him finding Cinderella, she'd slammed the door in his face.

How could she know if she loved him? She'd never experienced romantic love. Not with anyone. Was that what she felt for Jean-Philippe? Was love the cause of her elation when she was with him and the crushing emptiness when they were apart? Or was it how, when something important happened, her first thought was to tell Jean-Philippe about it?

Was that love?

How was she to know?

Love should be forever. When a person says they love someone, they're talking about forever. Of course love can die or change. But the words, "I love you," carried with them the hope of forever.

And the hope that the other person felt the same way.

If she dared to open her heart to Jean-Philippe, it would be forever. She knew there would be no turning back. But did she dare?

She found herself at the river. To her surprise, Luke was there.

"What are you doing here this time of day?" she asked as she approached him. For the first time she realized he wore the exact same outfit as the day they had first met, just as he had every day.

He had been standing and watching the river flow by. He smiled as he faced her. "I've come to say goodbye. The family is leaving."

She was stunned. "What? Why?"

"It's time," he said with a small smile. "And we're happy to go."

"I don't understand."

"That's all right. I wouldn't expect you to." His gaze lifted to the mountains, the sky. "But we've been here a long, long time, and finally we—I—learned what I needed to know. And it's filled me with joy."

His words only confused her. "What do you mean? What did you learn?"

But instead of answering, he smiled. "It's time, Julia. I'm

happy I got to know you. You, even more than the others in your family, have needed to be strong. You always have been, and you will continue to be. But now it's time for you also to be brave."

"I don't understand," she cried, and for some reason, the thought of him leaving her brought sudden tears to her eyes.

He smiled. "Those tears are good. It means you're opening your heart, letting yourself feel emotions you need to feel. Emotions like love."

"I was just thinking about how I don't really know what that is."

"I don't believe that. You know, but it still scares you. Remember what you said after you read my ... Hannah Donnelly's letter?" He paused, then added, "It's time, as I said, for you to be brave. Like she was."

She remembered—she said she admired Hannah. Hannah loved, and she took a chance. But how could Luke have known that? And then it all became clear. *My mother. He almost called Hannah his mother.*

"You have a big heart," he said, "but you've protected it long enough. Now, trust it, set it free, let it blossom. It's time for you to face all life has to offer."

"I don't know if I dare," she whispered.

"Being strong doesn't mean you need to be alone, Julia."

With that, he started walking away.

"Wait, Luke," she called. It was too soon. She wasn't ready to say goodbye yet. "I'm going to miss you."

But he didn't look back, and then she saw the little calico cat, Pumpkin, run up to him and walk along at his heels. The two must have turned a corner in the path she didn't know was there because, suddenly, they were gone. She knew she'd never see them again.

She walked over to the log where she and Luke had spent so much time talking.

Propped against the log was the portable easel she'd given him. She went over to it. The canvas was there as well, its back facing her. She picked it up and turned it over expecting to see the portrait of his nurse.

But the canvas was bare—as untouched as the day she'd bought it for him.

"No!" she said. Had he bought another? Gotten a replacement for the one she'd given him? But why would he do that?

She definitely recognized the easel stand—she'd carried it often enough for him. She opened it to the inside compartment for paints. The paints were all unopened. The brushes untouched.

She ran back to the cabin.

Her sketch book remained on the coffee table. She picked it up and turned to the page where Luke had sketched his nurse. The sketch was gone.

And when she looked up at Elijah Donnelly's portrait, his eyes no longer seemed to follow her.

She sat on the sofa. Otis came over to her and lay down at her side. "You lost your friend, Pumpkin, didn't you?" she whispered.

He snuggled closer.

CHAPTER 25

Julia sat in the cabin a long time. Luke had once said to her that there was much more in this world than we can ever understand, despite all our so-called knowledge and science. And Jean-Philippe said something similar—that his Grandmere believed the separation between this world and the other was a thin veil. And the way he said it made her think he felt much the same.

They were correct. It was all true. The ghosts, the family history. All of it.

It made sense now. And when Luke said he had learned what he needed to, she knew he was talking about Claire and Adele. He couldn't rest until he knew what had happened to them, and now he did.

She wondered if Elijah and Hannah weren't here to support him on his lonely quest, in the way they never could in life.

If she was right about that, she was glad he finally learned all about his child, and she couldn't help but believe he also saw his great-grandson.

Her thoughts turned, as they always seemed to these days, to

Jean-Philippe. Being with him ... she shook her head. She couldn't remember ever laughing so much, or acting so much out of character. Dancing, even singing. She scarcely knew herself.

But there was so much more as she thought of the risk he took rescuing the falcon from its trap, the danger he faced staring down Deon at the cabin as he did what he could to protect her. And then, helping her face her father, helping her past the man's rejection of her. He didn't have to do any of it, particularly not the last part—but he'd done it all for others.

Being with him—yes, even when circumstances had become dangerous—he brought something to her life she'd never experienced. Just seeing him each morning made the day come alive. And watching the clock as the day grew late, knowing in her heart, even if she didn't admit it, that he would soon return, had brought a spring to her step.

Being with him—she loved every moment. She loved ... him.

And she hoped she wasn't too late.

She hurried back to the area where she'd left him, but she didn't see him anywhere.

He had turned toward the rise when he walked away from her, and so she rushed to the gravesites, thinking he might still be there. But he wasn't. She saw that more weeds had been cleared around the graves. They had said they'd do that together. Yes—she had to laugh at herself—she even looked forward to clearing weeds with him. Truly, she must be in love.

She kept going to higher ground knowing that there, she would get a broad view of the land, their land, and maybe be able to see him somewhere close.

Not until she neared a tiny rivulet that in the spring would carry water from high snows down to the river, did she see him sitting on a rocky ledge, staring out at the field before him.

"Jean-Philippe," she called, hurrying toward him.

He faced her, his eyes questioning and for a moment, bright. But then he stiffened. "I'll leave soon." He turned his head away.

She saw the emptiness in his eyes before he averted them. She continued toward him.

"I've been sitting here telling myself that you were right," he said when she reached his side. "It was ridiculous of me to think I could fall in love with someone and decide to turn my entire life upside down—buy land, start a horse ranch, convince a fine but cautious woman to become my wife—all in a matter of weeks. What was I thinking? I've always been very prudent, even wary, about making any changes in life. But here, I've thrown caution to the wind. I must have been hit with some kind of madness."

"No, Jean-Philippe," she said, placing her hand on his arm.

"I decided I must have been caught up in the myth of the cabin's ghosts," he said with a wry smile. "I thought they purposefully had thrown the two of us together, knowing we would fall in love. But that would have nothing to do with real feelings. It's magic, enchantment—not anything for practical people like you and me."

An ache came over her, and she knew she would forever regret it if they walked away from each other now. A tightness filled her throat and chest as she struggled to find the right words. "You've always told me I'm a strong person. But someone wise told me I also need to be brave."

His eyes turned curious.

"I'll admit, it's hard for me," she said. "But I know that it's brave to open one's heart and take chances, brave to allow oneself to love when there are no assurances. The brave thing, feeling as I do about you, is to try to make things right, and hope for the best."

She waited, praying he understood. But he remained silent.

She couldn't help but turn her head and lift her gaze to the skies as if seeking help.

But instead, she saw something...

"Oh, my! Look," she cried, her voice filled with awe as she pointed at the sky.

Above them, a white gyrfalcon, the one Luke had called an arctic bird, circled and soared. They watched it land on a high branch of a fir tree near the cabin.

"That must be the one you saw the other day," Jean-Philippe murmured, his eyes never leaving the bird. "She's wonderful! Her being still here may mean she likes the area and will stay throughout the winter."

"And she's safe thanks to you," Julia said. "Without you, she might have been trapped."

"You helped," he added.

"Without you, I, too, was trapped—trapped in my own fears. I protected myself so well, I forgot about living, about loving. I'm not good expressing myself. It's easier to walk away, but I don't want to do that. I'm don't want to lose you." Her words were heartfelt.

He faced her, his eyes hopeful. "Are you sure? Are you sure this is about us and not just the cabin's ghosts and their matchmaking?"

The wind blew a lock of hair onto his forehead. She reached up and brushed it back from his brow. "Can't it be both? I think somehow they brought you here. But now, they've gone. Luke said he has the answers he needed, and they're happy to go." She stared at him. "And I know he couldn't be more proud of his great-grandson."

He shut his eyes a moment as her words filled him. Then, he searched her face. "You give me hope, *Julie*," he said.

"The ghosts are gone. They did as much as they could, and

it's now up to us," she said. "I love you, Jean-Philippe. I love you so very much."

"That's what I've needed to hear from you," he whispered. "I love you, and I always will."

She kissed him, a kiss filled with the passion she'd kept buried inside for so long. He returned the kiss with all the ardor, devotion, and love she'd spent a lifetime waiting for, waiting until she met the one man she dared to trust, the one man she could love.

She had spent a lifetime looking for a place to call home. But not until that moment did she realize that it wasn't the place that made a home, but the one very special person in it. In his arms, be it at the cabin, on his future horse ranch, or wherever life might take them, as long as they were together, she would always be home.

PLUS ...

Dear Reader,

I hope you've enjoyed this romance with a touch of ghostly fantasy. I've written other romances as well as a number of romantic mysteries.

To find out about more of my books, please join my mailing list at www.joannepence.com.

One of the best loved of my contemporary romances is Seems Like Old Times. For your enjoyment, here's Chapter 1:

Seems Like Old Times

The low-lying redwood and glass buildings of Miwok High stood on the opposite side of the creek. As Lee Reynolds, news anchor on a national cable television network, pulled into the parking lot, she saw that the school was empty, the gates shut. She hadn't been back here since she had left town during the summer following her high school graduation, seventeen years earlier.

She got out of the car. The door slamming shut was like a

rifle crack in the quiet. A wooden Japanese-style arced foot-
bridge crossed over the creek to the school buildings, and along
its banks weeping willows bowed their branches.

Lee stepped toward the bridge, then stopped. A part of her
wanted to hurry away, warned her that being here was playing
Russian roulette with her memories. But another, stronger part
pushed her closer to the school. She crossed over the rippling
waters of the creek.

The air was unnaturally still as if, could she but listen hard
enough, she would hear the bustling and laughter of students
past and present, hear whispers of secrets shared and promises
broken.

A lone bicycle rider cut in front of her, dropped his blue bike
off at the bicycle rack, climbed over the cyclone fence
surrounding the school, and disappeared between the buildings.
Amused, Lee watched his every movement, wondering what
could possibly cause a teenage boy to break *into* his school
grounds on a Saturday afternoon. Thoughts of burglary and
vandalism came to mind because of stories she heard every day
living in Manhattan, but she quickly dismissed them. This was
Miwok, California, after all, a small rural town forty miles
north of San Francisco. The boy had probably forgotten a
homework assignment.

She wasn't about to hop a fence. As she turned to leave, her
gaze caught the blue bicycle.

Tony Santos had a bike that color....

She shuddered, then slid her hands into the pockets of her
linen jacket and began to stroll along the dirt path that circled
the outside perimeter of the school.

She glanced back at the bike once more, wistful yet
surprised at how sharply her memories had returned. The first
time she'd ever seen Tony he was standing beside his bike, right
about where the boy left his. Lee had been waiting for her best

friend, Cheryl McConnell. She was fifteen, a sophomore, and Tony was the same. He'd been bending over the bicycle rack, working the combination lock. As he yanked the lock and chain off his bike, he noticed her watching him and straightened, allowing the chain to hang against his long legs. Then he smiled.

She shook her head slightly at the memory. He'd burst into her quiet world with all the charged energy and motion of a sonic boom. He had charm. She'd never forget his charm. Or his independence. Or his knowledge of the world beyond Miwok. She'd envied that knowledge with all her heart, and had ached to see that world, away from Miwok, away from her widowed mother, and to become a part of it.

She had heard about Tony since the first day he showed up in class, which wasn't surprising in a school of only three hundred students. He was Mexican, and no other Mexican kids went to Miwok High. Most lived inside the town limits on the other side of the valley and went to Drake, an older, far larger school. But Tony Santos' father worked and lived out at the Circle Z Ranch, so he was in Miwok's school district.

The other kids said he was quiet. Maybe he didn't know English, they snickered, and he didn't seem to have any money. They decided his father probably cleaned the stables and that Tony Santos was, in short, a nobody.

How pompous those kids were. And she was one of the worst. How rudely she'd stared at him there, at the school's entrance.

Thin and lanky, he seemed to be all arms, legs and feet. His black hair was straight and shiny, and the forelock that fell as he bent over the bike reached past his eyes. A high, narrow nose flared slightly at the nostrils; deep-set brown eyes peered under arched brows; and a finely shaped mouth curved upward. His skin was a light olive tone, yet shades darker than hers. As her stare continued, his smile faded, and he stared back, his chin arrogantly lifted.

He took a step toward her. The bicycle chain still hung from his fingers. She stiffened. She had heard Mexican kids were always fighting and getting into trouble with the law. At his next step she jumped back, ready to run.

He froze, then turned his back to her as he lifted his book bag onto his shoulders. Sliding the bike off the rack, he swung one leg over it in a smooth, graceful motion, then standing as he pedaled he rode right past her through the open gate, never meeting her gaze. He reached the street and sped down it.

Tony Santos...

She felt a chill. Ghosts of the past really must dwell here, she thought. Either that or the weather was turning cold.

She couldn't believe how far she had walked. She reached the backside of the school, past the classrooms and in view of the playing fields. The grounds were enormous, almost like those of a private college or university. Swathed in lawns they included a field for football and another for baseball.

When had she stopped going to baseball games?

The chain-linked backstop, shaped like a giant bustle, jutted into the sky and drew her toward it.

Her gaze drifted from the pitcher's mound, to the diamond, the outfield fence, then back to the stands and the announcer's booth. Something about a baseball field, even when it was empty, echoed the crack of a bat, the roaring cheers of a crowd.

She had sat untold hours in the stands watching Tony. She could almost see him once again looking slender but strong in his blue and white uniform standing at home plate, his knees slightly bent, leaning forward at the waist, elbows out, a powerful grip on the bat held high over his right shoulder. A royal blue cap with a white "M" on its crown shaded eyes that stared unflinchingly at the pitcher.

She turned to go home. The image faded, but the memory of the boy lingered. She bowed her head, her pulse drumming, not believing that after so many years the remembrance could be so sharp. Or so painful.

Continue with Seems Like Old Times wherever fine books or ebooks are sold.

ABOUT THE AUTHOR

Joanne Pence was born and raised in northern California. She has been an award-winning, *USA Today* best-selling author of mysteries for many years, but she has also written historical fiction, contemporary romance, romantic suspense, a fantasy, and supernatural suspense. All of her books are now available as ebooks and in print, and most are also offered in special large print editions. Joanne hopes you'll enjoy her books, which present a variety of times, places, and reading experiences, from mysterious to thrilling, emotional to lightly humorous, as well as powerful tales of times long past.

Visit her at www.joannepence.com and be sure to sign up for Joanne's mailing list to hear about new books.

Contemporary, Fantasy, and Historical Romance

Seems Like Old Times

When Lee Reynolds, nationally known television news anchor, returns to the small town where she was born to sell her now-vacant childhood home, little does she expect to find that her first love has moved back to town. Nor does she expect that her feelings for him are still so strong.

Tony Santos had been a major league baseball player, but now finds his days of glory gone. He's gone back home to raise his young son as a single dad.

Both Tony and Lee have changed a lot. Yet, being with him, she finds that in her heart, it seems like old times...

The Ghost of Squire House

For decades, the home built by reclusive artist, Paul Squire, has stood empty on a windswept cliff overlooking the ocean. Those who attempted to live in the home soon fled in terror. Jennifer Barrett knows nothing of the history of the house she inherited. All she knows is she's glad for the chance to make a new life for herself.

It's Paul Squire's duty to rid his home of intruders, but something about this latest newcomer's vulnerable status ... and resemblance of someone from his past ... dulls his resolve. Jennifer would like to find a real flesh-and-blood man to liven her days and nights—someone to share her life with—but living in the artist's house, studying his paintings, she is surprised at how close she feels to him.

A compelling, prickly ghost with a tortured, guilt-ridden past, and a lonely heroine determined to start fresh, find themselves in a battle of wills and emotion in this ghostly fantasy of love, time, and chance.

Dangerous Journey

C.J. Perkins is trying to find her brother who went missing while on a Peace Corps assignment in Asia. All she knows is that the disappearance has something to do with a "White Dragon." Darius Kane, adventurer and bounty hunter, seems to be her only hope, and she practically shanghais him into helping her.

With a touch of the romantic adventure film Romancing the Stone, C.J. and Darius follow a trail that takes them through the narrow streets of Hong Kong, the backrooms of San Francisco's Chinatown, and the wild jungles of Borneo as they pursue both her brother and the White Dragon. The closer C.J. gets to them, the more danger she finds herself in—and it's not just danger of losing her life, but also of losing her heart.

Dance with a Gunfighter

Gabriella Devere wants vengeance. She grows up quickly when she witnesses the murder of her family by a gang of outlaws, and vows to make them pay for their crime. When the law won't help her, she takes matters into her own hands.

Jess McLowry left his war-torn Southern home to head West, where he hired out his gun. When he learns what happened to Gabriella's family, and what she plans, he knows a young woman like her will have no chance against the outlaws, and vows to save her the way he couldn't save his own family.

But the price of vengeance is high and Gabriella's willingness to sacrifice everything ultimately leads to the book's deadly and startling conclusion.

Willa Cather Literary Award finalist for Best Historical Novel.

The Dragon's Lady

Turn-of-the-century San Francisco comes to life in this romance of star-crossed lovers whose love is forbidden by both society and the laws of the time.

Ruth Greer, wealthy daughter of a shipping magnate, finds a young boy who has run away from his home in Chinatown—an area of gambling parlors, opium dens, and sing-song girls, as well as families trying to eke out a living. It is also home to the infamous and deadly "hatchet men" of Chinese lore.

There, Ruth meets Li Han-lin, a handsome, enigmatic leader of one such tong, and discovers he is neither as frightening cruel, or wanton as reputation would have her believe. As Ruth's fascination with the lawless area grows, she finds herself pulled deeper into its intrigue and dangers, particularly those surrounding Han-lin. But the two are from completely different worlds, and when both worlds are shattered by the Great Earthquake and Fire of 1906 that destroyed most of San Francisco, they face their ultimate test.

The Cabin of Love & Magic Romances

Three half-sisters inherit a remote cabin, but there's just one problem with it. It's haunted.

IF I LOVED YOU
THIS CAN'T BE LOVE
SENTIMENTAL JOURNEY

The Rebecca Mayfield Mysteries

Rebecca is a by-the-book detective, who walks the straight and narrow in her work, and in her life. Richie, on the other hand, is not at all by-the-book. But opposites can and do attract, and there are few mystery two-somes quite as opposite as Rebecca and Richie.

ONE O'CLOCK HUSTLE – North American Book Award winner in Mystery
TWO O'CLOCK HEIST
THREE O'CLOCK SÉANCE
FOUR O'CLOCK SIZZLE
FIVE O'CLOCK TWIST
SIX O'CLOCK SILENCE
Plus a Christmas Novella: The Thirteenth Santa

The Angie & Friends Food & Spirits Mysteries

Angie Amalfi and Homicide Inspector Paavo Smith are soon to be married in this latest mystery series. Crime and calories plus a new "twist" in Angie's life in the form of a ghostly family inhabiting the house she and Paavo buy, create a mystery series with a "spirited" sense of fun and adventure.

COOKING SPIRITS

ADD A PINCH OF MURDER

COOK'S BIG DAY

Plus a Christmas mystery-fantasy: COOK'S CURIOUS CHRISTMAS

And a cookbook: COOK'S DESSERT COOKBOOK

The early "Angie Amalfi mystery series" began when Angie first met San Francisco Homicide Inspector Paavo Smith. Here are those mysteries in the order written:

SOMETHING'S COOKING

TOO MANY COOKS

COOKING UP TROUBLE

COOKING MOST DEADLY

COOK'S NIGHT OUT

COOKS OVERBOARD

A COOK IN TIME

TO CATCH A COOK

BELL, COOK, AND CANDLE

IF COOKS COULD KILL

TWO COOKS A-KILLING

COURTING DISASTER

RED HOT MURDER

THE DA VINCI COOK

Supernatural Suspense

Ancient Echoes

Top Idaho Fiction Book Award Winner

Over two hundred years ago, a covert expedition shadowing Lewis and Clark disappeared in the wilderness of Central

Idaho. Now, seven anthropology students and their professor vanish in the same area. The key to finding them lies in an ancient secret, one that men throughout history have sought to unveil.

Michael Rempart is a brilliant archeologist with a colorful and controversial career, but he is plagued by a sense of the supernatural and a spiritual intuitiveness. Joining Michael are a CIA consultant on paranormal phenomena, a washed-up local sheriff, and a former scholar of Egyptology. All must overcome their personal demons as they attempt to save the students and learn the expedition's terrible secret....

Ancient Shadows

One by one, a horror film director, a judge, and a newspaper publisher meet brutal deaths. A link exists between them, and the deaths have only begun ....

Archeologist Michael Rempart finds himself pitted against ancient demons and modern conspirators when a dying priest gives him a powerful artifact—a pearl said to have granted Genghis Khan the power, eight centuries ago, to lead his Mongol warriors across the steppes to the gates of Vienna.

The artifact has set off centuries of war and destruction as it conjures demons to play upon men's strongest ambitions and cruelest desires. Michael realizes the so-called pearl is a philosopher's stone, the prime agent of alchemy. As much as he would like to ignore the artifact, when he sees horrific deaths and experiences, first-hand, diabolical possession and affliction, he has no choice but to act, to follow a path along the Old Silk Road to a land that time forgot, and to somehow find a place that may no longer exist in the world as he knows it.

Ancient Illusions

A long-lost diary, a rare book of ghost stories, and unrelenting